UNTAMED DADDY
MOUNTAIN MEN OF BEAR VALLEY

CHANTEL SEABROOK

FRANKIE LOVE

CHAPTER 1

eston

"Dammit, Finley, where are you?" I growl out, trying my best to stay calm and not freak the fuck out.

Last time she snuck off I told her it needed to be the last. But here I am, once again, running down Main Street calling out for my little girl. Finley may be six, but the kid acts like she's going on sixteen, and I need to put a stop to her reckless behavior before something happens to her.

"Finley? You are in so much trouble when I find you," I call, feeling the tug of fear course through me. If I were in the woods right now, I'd shift into bear form - run with all my might, let out a growl that would tell my daughter she crossed the line - that it is time to stay within her father's line of sight. But I can't exactly do that here in the open, on the main drag of Bear Valley.

And Finley knows that. She's testing my boundaries more than she ought. If she had a mother, maybe it wouldn't be like this - me being both mother and father to her. That dream died along with her mom though.

"What are you hollering about?" Bennett, my younger brother, asks, crossing the street with a sandwich from the deli.

"It's Fin, I can't find her." I run a hand over my beard, my eyes darting around. "She's gonna be the end of me."

"She can't have gone far," Bennett says, following me as I head down the sidewalk, brushing past tourists as I move quickly. "She was sitting on the bench outside the guide shop before I left to get lunch."

"Yeah?" I say crossly. "Well, she's a little girl. *My little girl.* And there's an entire Grizzly clan out for revenge."

"The Grizzlies aren't insane enough to put a child in the crossfire of this..." He struggles to find the word.

"This fuckup?" I suggest as we hustle down the street together.

Bennett shakes his head. "I was gonna say feud."

"You're always such a damn diplomat." I stop running, seeing a whip of wild blonde hair through the window of the bookstore cafe. "Thank God."

Bennett claps me on the back. "See, she's fine. She walked down the street and—"

"She's not fine," I cut him off as I pull open the door to the shop. "She needs to learn boundaries before something happens to her."

As I step inside to deal with my adorable yet unruly daughter, Bennett calls to me as he walks away. "Don't be too hard on her, after all, she takes after you."

I grunt, knowing it's the truth.

Stepping inside the shop, my nostrils fill with the most insane scent. Vanilla bean wafts around me as I move toward the kitchen, where I hear a very recognizable giggle. Bennett's words echo in my ear. I was unruly and gave my poor mother a run for her money. I always played by my own rules, marched to the beat of my own drum - but I learned my lesson. When I hooked up with Heidi, Finley's mother, I never intended things to go sideways so fast. But they did.

I won't make that mistake again. Not with any woman.

"Daddy!" Finley cries as I enter the kitchen where a batch of cookies has just been pulled from the oven. She's sitting cross-legged on the counter as if she owns the place. "What are you doing here?"

She looks upset to see me, her eyebrows furrowed and her waist-length hair a knot of messy waves, unruly, just like the flash of emotion in her eyes.

Kate, the resident baker of this little cafe, gives me a small shrug of her shoulders as she begins removing the cookies from the sheet and setting them carefully on a cooling rack. When she drops a potholder, I can't help but look her over as she bends down to pick it up. Her round ass has me swallowing hard - this is the last thing I need. A distraction.

I need to focus on getting my little girl in line. Especially since Finley seems to have no concern for rules.

In fact, she takes a spoon from a bowl of cookie dough and begins eating from it.

"Hey," I say, taking the spoon from her. "What do you think you're doing?"

Finley gives me a mischievous smile. "Having a snack with Kate, Daddy. Gosh!"

I glance over at Kate who bites back a smile. Her red hair is piled on the top of her head, set in place with a pencil, and her black apron is dusted with flour. Somehow, she looks exactly at home in this kitchen, which is surprising. I always hear how she is in Alaska to write a book, yet she looks so comfortable with the spatula in her hand. In fact, she looks really fucking hot.

I feel frazzled - being in this kitchen. I shouldn't be here. And neither should Finley.

"You, missy, ran off without permission," I say, turning my attention to my daughter, refusing to let my little girl's upturned nose and spattering of freckles deter my lecture. "I told you this was the last time. No ice cream this afternoon, understood?"

Finley jumps from the counter, crossing her arms. "That's not fair."

Ignoring her protest, I tell her to wash up in the bathroom, and thankfully with a huff, she obeys.

I look over at Kate, she's twisting her lips like she has something on her mind.

"There something you want to say?" I ask. "Because you know, you shouldn't have let her back here without telling me. I was worried sick."

She lifts her eyebrows. "Oh, this is my fault?"

"I didn't mean—"

"Look," Kate says, taking a cookie and breaking it in two. She hands me half and takes a bite. "She told me she asked you if she could hang out while you finished up work."

"And?" I ask. "I know women well enough to know you have a few more thoughts on the matter."

She snorts. "If you must know, the consequence of no ice cream this afternoon is pretty lame."

I scowl. "What do you know about parenting?"

"I know enough from helping with my nieces and nephews, from babysitting for like, a decade, to know that if she really ran down here without permission, she doesn't seem to understand boundaries. That's scary, Weston."

I see the concern in her eyes, and her words don't carry any judgment, even if she thinks it. Kate isn't vindictive. She's making cookies with my little girl for heaven's sake. Even if she is young, the woman has more motherly instincts in her left pinkie then most of the women in this damn valley combined. Not that I've been looking for a mother for Fin, but I've gone through enough babysitters to know it takes someone special to spend a day with my little girl and not want to pull their hair out by the end of it.

A thought comes to me.

"Then why don't you spend more time with her?" I take a bite of the cookie she offered. Damn, it's as good as it smells.

I wonder if Kate tastes just as good.

Shit. I push the thought away.

"You think you can teach her some boundaries? She seems to listen to you."

"You're the parent, not me," she says, setting her hand on my arm. I feel a spark at her touch and our eyes meet, and she quickly pulls her hand back and glances away, returning to her baking. She gives a small shrug. "I didn't mean to insinuate I could do a better job. You're a good dad, Weston."

For a moment the kitchen goes quiet. I've never spent much time with Kate, she is always quiet, shy, but here in this kitchen, it's like she is more relaxed. I like this side of her.

The woman is beautiful, but she doesn't seem to know it. I've never had a thing for redheads, but the color, a dark shade of auburn, fits her perfectly. She always has it up in a bun or a ponytail, but I can't help wondering what it would look like down, draped over her bare shoulders, across her milky skin as she—

"Weston?" Kate is looking at me expectantly like she's asked a question.

Shit. I clear my throat.

"I could use the help," I admit, rubbing the back of my neck, and trying to stay focused on why I came in here - Finley.

"Look," Kate adds with a small sigh. "If she wants to stay

and help me clean up this mess, then that is fine by me. But I don't want to step on any toes."

"You wouldn't be." I hold her gaze, probably longer than I should, but there's something about the blue of her eyes that has me mesmerized. She's not just pretty, there's also a sweetness to her, edged with a strength that's hidden under her shyness.

She's the opposite of Heidi, who was always wanting to be the center of attention, finding her confidence in the way others saw her. She'd been beautiful, and full of life, and even though she wasn't my mate, I'd let myself fall hard for her.

And then I'd lost her.

The day that should have been the happiest of my life had turned into heartbreak. Holding my newborn daughter in my arms, I'd been rushed from the delivery room, not knowing what was happening.

She'd hemorrhaged on the table. There was nothing they could do. No one to blame. But I knew the truth. It was our punishment for going against the laws of the bears.

Heidi wasn't my mate, but she was someone else's.

Axel. The man went crazy when she denied him. Or maybe he was insane before. It's hard to know, since the grizzlies aren't exactly stable to begin with.

He'd tried to kill Finley. And he would have if my brother and his mate hadn't been there to protect her. The man is dead now, but that doesn't mean the threat is over.

Heidi came from the Grizzly clan, which makes my daughter both Kodiak and Grizzly. And those insane bears think that she somehow belongs to them. They've already made a couple of attempts to kidnap her.

And while I don't think they'll dare set foot on Kodiak territory for some time, after the council ordered them to stay away, I still worry.

But how the hell do you explain to a six-year-old that

there is an entire clan of bears that want to snatch her away, without scaring the shit out of her?

"Daddy, are you going to leave now?" Finley asks, staring up at me, arms crossed. I'd been so lost in my thoughts I hadn't noticed she'd come back into the room.

Kate is watching me still, and I see a flash of concern in her eyes.

But Finley just taps her toes, obviously impatient that I'm still here.

"What? You don't want to hang out with your dad?"

"Kate is way more fun."

"Really?" I glance over at the woman, who's holding back a smile. "And why's that?"

"Because she makes cookies, and tells stories, and she doesn't turn into a bear when she's mad—"

"Finley," I say sharply. She knows better than to mention the bear-thing around others.

"What?" She blinks up at me all innocent-like, which I know is an act. The kid is pushing my buttons.

"You know the rules. You can stay with Kate if you're going to follow them."

She sighs. "Okay."

Kate is watching us, brows furrowed. Even though two of her closest friends are mated to my brothers, as far as I'm aware, she doesn't know about our kind. And for all of our sakes, it's best it stays that way.

"I can get a little grumpy sometimes," I say, trying to cover my tracks. "I don't actually turn into a bear."

Kate gives a small laugh. "I didn't think you did. But wouldn't that be something to see."

"Yeah." I chuckle uneasily.

"I'll bring her home after dinner," Kate says, shooing me out of the kitchen.

"You're sure you don't mind watching her?" I glance over

at Finley, who's already climbed up on one of the stools and is elbow deep in flour.

"With Harley and Adelaide gone, it'll be nice to have the company." A flash of what looks like loneliness tugs at her features.

That's one emotion I understand all too well. I have Finley and my brothers, but it's not the same as having someone to share your life with. But loneliness is a small price to pay for not experiencing the pain of loss and heartbreak.

"Okay." I'm not sure why I'm having such a hard time walking away. I should be grateful that I have the afternoon off, to get some work done without worrying about where Finley has wandered off to. "I guess I'll see you later."

"She'll be fine," Kate says, obviously thinking that's the reason for my hesitation.

Good. It's better than her knowing the thoughts I'd had about her earlier. How if Finley wasn't here, I may just be tempted to pull the woman into my arms and kiss her.

Big mistake, my brain warns.

What I need is to get laid. It's been too damn long. That's the only reason I'm feeling all mixed up inside about the pretty little redhead with lips that would look so damn good wrapped around my cock.

Shit.

I turn and walk away before the woman notices the damn hard-on I'm sporting, or before I do something stupid, like ask her out on a date.

Not only is she my brothers' mates' best friend, but she's also not the kind of woman who does casual sex. And right now, that's all I have to offer. No emotions. No commitment. Just a night of pleasure that will have her toes curling and crying out my name in ecstasy.

I may be practically abstinent, but there are some things a man doesn't forget how to do.

As I leave the kitchen, I turn and give Kate one last look. Turns out, she's still looking at me, with a look in her eyes that can only be described as hunger - even though she has a dozen cookies right there on the counter.

Maybe I was wrong.

Maybe Kate can handle a no-strings night together.

CHAPTER 2

ate

"Can't I sleep over at your place?" Finley asks as I take her hand and walk down Main Street toward the two-story house with the white picket fence that seems completely at odds with the man who owns it.

Finley's earlier comment about her dad turning into a bear when he gets upset didn't surprise me. The man is all growlly and wild one minute, looking like he's ready to devour me, and the next he's all sullen and moody.

"I'll be good, I promise," Finley says, skipping beside me.

"How about this, you be good for your dad. No more running off without telling him, and we'll talk about having a sleepover."

"You can sleep over at my place."

I cough, wondering what Weston would think of his daughter's offer. The man is so hard to read. I know only the little bit of information about him that Adelaide has shared.

Like his brothers, he helps run the guide shop. As far as I know, he was never married to Finley's mom, but they were engaged, and according to Harley, they were crazy in love. And he hasn't dated anyone since the woman passed away.

I get it.

Probably better than most.

I've loved and lost. Experienced tragedy like a knife to the heart. Matt was the only boy I ever truly cared about. Everyone said we were too young to know what real love was, that it would never last, and they were right.

I just never expected it to end the way it did.

One drunk driver, and my life was forever changed. I should have been in the car with him that night, but we'd had an argument. It was stupid and petty, and I can't even remember now what started it, all I know is that the last words I said to him were out of anger.

I inhale a deep breath and let it out, blinking back tears that I never let fall.

Three years. It should be enough time for the pain to subside, but it still catches me unaware every once in a while.

"Are you sad?" Finley asks, taking my hand.

"I was just thinking about someone that I miss."

She twists her lips and I can see the wheels spinning in her head. "Sometimes I miss my mommy even though I never met her."

"I'm sorry she's not here with you." I give her small hand a squeeze, wondering if that isn't one of the reasons she's been acting out.

"Who do you miss?"

"A boy I once loved."

"Where is he?"

I glance up at the sky, then back at her. "Up in heaven."

"Like my mommy."

"Yeah."

"Maybe they're watching over us together."

I smile. "Maybe."

"There you are." Weston comes out on the porch when we start up the steps of the house.

"Kate said I can have a sleepover at her place," Finley says, jumping up and down until he picks her up.

He raises a brow at me. "She did, huh?"

"Yeah. And we're going to make cupcakes and I get to decorate them."

"Sounds like fun." He puts her down when she squirms in his arms.

The girl is a ball of energy.

"I'm going to tell Baloo," she says before scurrying into the house.

"Baloo?"

"Her cat." Weston rubs the back of his neck and leans on the door frame.

"Like the bear from the Jungle Book?"

"You watch Disney movies?"

I shrug. "Like I said, I have a lot of nieces and nephews. But to be honest, I never really got over the whole princess thing."

He chuckles. "I don't see you as a princess."

I frown, suddenly feeling very self-conscious. I tuck a strand of my wild red hair behind my ear. "What do you see me as?"

"It was a compliment, Kate." He takes a step toward me. "You don't seem like a woman who's looking for her Prince Charming to make her happy."

I swallow, because he's close now, and a warmth spreads through my core. "I learned a long time ago not to hope for a happily ever after, but that doesn't mean I don't want one."

I still wish for one. And even though Weston's right in a

way, that I'm not looking for a man to complete me, there's still a part of me that hopes one day to share my life with someone. My girlfriends tease me about it, they assume I'm a hopeless romantic - it's more than that though. I believe in love because I've experienced it.

And deep down I want to experience it again.

There's also the part of me that wants something I don't even understand, that I've never had, and have only read about in romance novels - to be completely ravished.

"So, what are you looking for?" he asks, leaning closer, studying me like he can read my thoughts.

"I...uh..." I take a step back, forgetting that there are steps behind me.

Before I fall, Weston reaches out, wrapping a large arm around my waist, and pulls me toward him. "Careful."

I swear to God, I moan when my palms flatten on his chest. Holy shit, the man is ripped. And even though he's right, and I've never wanted to be the whole damsel in distress needing a white knight to save me, it feels good to be held by powerful arms, to feel...safe.

But more than that, I feel something stir inside of me. A hunger. A need. Like my body has been in a deep sleep, and all I need is one kiss to wake it up completely.

Like I said earlier, I never got over the whole princess thing.

Weston is still holding me, dark eyes piercing and primal, and I swear I hear a growl rumble in his chest.

"You didn't answer my question," he says roughly.

"Wha-what question?" I stutter, unable to pull my gaze away from his mouth that's just inches from mine.

"What do you want, Kate?"

You. Your body on mine. In mine. Filling me. Taking me. Pushing me to limits I've only dreamed about.

I whimper, and it must be enough of an answer because his mouth crashes against mine, and he kisses me with a wildness that makes every cell in my body come alive.

CHAPTER 3

 eston

ONE KISS. ONE FUCKING KISS IS ALL IT TAKES.

This woman, Kate - she's mine. I press my lips against hers, suddenly starved. Her mouth opens, my tongue swirls against hers. She tastes so sweet, like those damn vanilla bean cookies and I want more. Everything. Her. My cock strains against my blue jeans and her body leans into mine like it knows where it belongs.

"Daddy?" Finley shouts from the house. "I can't get the TV on!"

My daughter's cry from inside forces Kate to pull back, and I hate that the moment ended so damn soon, but hell, what am I thinking?

I'm supposed to focus on Finley, on getting her in line - not getting all hot and bothered over a woman much too sweet for me. Kate is all princess wishes and daydreams and I don't know what else - but I'm not it. She needs a fucking Prince Charming, not a Beast.

"Daddy!" Finley pushes open the front door screen. "You're not listening!" She stomps away, and I catch Kate's eyebrows as they fly up, as if surprised to see my little girl be so demanding.

"I take it you haven't seen Finley's tantrums yet?" I run a hand over my beard.

"No, she's a little precocious but never so ... "

"Loud?" I chuckle. "Thing is, Fin is my whole world, has been since the moment she was born. And she's an only grandchild to boot. To say she's spoiled is an understatement. Yet I just can't seem to say no."

Kate listens, not saying anything. Her pink tongue darting over her lips. My jaw tenses at the sight.

"Listen," I say. "It's been a long day, and I could use a cold drink. Wanna come in for a beer? As a thank you for hanging out with Fin."

She twists her lips, what she's debating I don't know. Finally, she says sure and follows me as I lead the way inside.

"Sorry, wasn't planning on company." I look around my cabin, trying to see it from Kate's perspective. The sink is full of dishes, a basket of unfolded laundry on the couch. Thumbtacks hold some posters in place, a poker table is pushed in a corner, piled high with old fishing gear I can't seem to part with.

Looking at Kate, I try to read her expression, but she seems nonplussed by my bachelor pad.

She steps over the boots piled around the front door as I push open the back door looking for Fin. She's abandoned getting the television to work and is in her teepee on the back porch, Baloo curled in a pile of blankets.

"That's Finley's fort?" Kate asks.

I nod. "Yeah, I promised her a treehouse though and need to get on it. She's pretty much outgrown that thing."

"Winter is coming shortly, isn't it?" Kate asks, following me back inside. "It's going to be dark most of the day, right?"

I smirk. "You saying I'll be out of time soon?"

She smiles as I pull open the fridge. I pop the caps and hand her an IPA. "This okay?"

She nods. "I'm not so picky."

"I always thought you were kinda … prissy."

She moans softly. "Gosh, that's some reputation I've garnered for myself here in Bear Valley."

I take a swig, realizing Kate is easier going than I gave her credit for. And it's a good thing. Because that kiss told me something pretty fucking important.

She's my mate.

I want to kiss Kate again, and I step toward her, prepared to make a move when Finley comes inside the house. "I'm hungry," she says. "Can we order pizza?"

"Uh sure." Looking over at Kate I add, "Want to stay for dinner?"

She shakes her head and sets down the beer. "Thanks for the invite, but I promised Addie I'd help her organize the nursery."

I nod, walking her out as Finley protests.

"I'll see you in the morning. Your dad will drop you off and we can make those cupcakes, okay?"

Finley seems pleased with this compromise.

Kate kneels, eye level with Finley. "But listen, sweet pea, you've got to be a big girl for your daddy tonight. That means taking a bath and brushing your hair without a fuss, tidy your bedroom before you turn out the lights, and maybe even tell your dad, that big ole' bear, to clean that kitchen of his."

Finley giggles at that, looking up at me. "You *are* a mess, Daddy."

Kate leans in. "True, but you're the lady of this house, Fin. I bet you can give him some chores."

Finley lets out a loud laugh, thinking this is the funniest idea she's ever heard.

Kate leaves down the front steps and I stand there with Finley's hand tucked in mine. We watch her go, both seemingly mesmerized by the woman.

"I like Kate a lot," Finley says.

I watch her go back toward town, thinking that she's really the complete fucking package. She is generous, can cook, can kiss like no one's business.

"I like her too, Fin."

It's the truth, but damn, there is no way in hell a woman like her would fall for a bear like me.

CHAPTER 4

ate

We're sitting on the carpeted floor of what will be Addie's son's nursery folding her tiny little baby clothes and sorting them into piles by type.

The room is painted blue with a dark wood crib and changing table. She hasn't had her baby shower yet, but I don't think she's going to need much. There are so many onesies in this room I lost count.

I told Addie I'd dropped Finley off at home earlier this evening and she has lots of opinions on her brother-in-law.

"His place is a mess, isn't it?" Addie asks.

"Yeah, it's pretty much a bachelor pad. But it doesn't really matter. He loves Finley, and that's what is important."

"Sure, but he gives Finley too much free rein. She needs more discipline. Structure. Boundaries. She runs away all the time, it stresses the whole family out."

I bite the side of my lip, feeling defensive of a father and daughter I barely know.

But I know something. At least, I know something about Weston's lips and how they feel against mine.

Perfect. God, the man can kiss. It was like my whole body was set on fire, and I'm pretty sure if Finley hadn't interrupted us, it would have turned into more. I hadn't realized how starved I was for a man's touch. But not just any man - Weston's touch.

"Well, I'll be hanging out with Finley tomorrow. I won't let her run away on me."

Addie frowns. "Why are you babysitting Finley on your day off? You said you were going to sequester yourself in your bedroom all day and work on your book."

I pick up a mint green sleeper printed with tiny little bears. Folding it, I answer, "She wanted to make cupcakes. It sounded fun."

The truth is my book sucks. I took a sabbatical from the bakery because I wanted a fresh start. But every time I try to write a chapter the characters feel flat and forced. Then I go in the kitchen and whip up a batch of blueberry scones and they come out perfect, light and airy and oh so good.

I can't help but wonder what exactly I'm trying to accomplish by giving up my career and moving to the middle of nowhere to become a novelist. As fun as it sounds, writing a romance novel isn't as easy as baking a flourless chocolate cake. At least not for me.

I love to read, that doesn't mean I love to write. Or am any good at it.

"Well that's nice of you," Addie says. "Finley could use some TLC. And if she's taken a liking to you, run with it. Whenever I've tried to spend time with her, she gets really wound up."

"She's still rambunctious with me."

Addie smiles. "Not surprised considering you feed her sugar the entire time you're together."

I laugh. "That's true. She has a penchant for sweets, just like me."

"And just like her dad. Weston has the sweet tooth of the family."

"Oh really?" I lick my lips, trying not to think about the kiss. How it was very sweet indeed.

"Do you..." Addie pauses. "Do you have a thing for Weston, Kate?"

I blanch. "What?" I shake my head, maybe a little too aggressively. "No way. We're opposites. He's a guy's-guy. Not my type at all. I've always been attracted to men who wear Dockers and play golf."

"Guys who play it safe you mean?"

"What's wrong with safe?" I ask, swallowing my emotions. The sad truth is, safe doesn't guarantee anything. I know that because Matt was a safe pick and he's gone.

Still, it seems less scary than a man like Weston.

"I know you've been waiting for your Prince Charming to sweep you off your feet." She shrugs, but I see a flash of light in her eyes. "But you know, Cinderella isn't the only fairy tale."

I shake my head, not following as Addie picks up another sleeper, this one printed with bears too. What's with that theme?

"Yeah," she continues, a smile that I can't quite interpret tugging at her lips, like she's in on a secret I don't know. "Maybe your love story is more Beauty and the Beast."

"This is so cool," Finley says as she lets the homemade

pink slime we just made slip through her small fingers. "Can we make purple now?"

"How about we get cleaned up and go outside? It's such a nice day out." Probably one of the last of the season. The leaves are already changing color and the days are growing shorter.

"What are you two doing in here?" Piper asks, coming into the kitchen, lifting a dark eyebrow at me when she sees Finley.

"We're making slime." Fin takes a big gob of it and places it in Piper's hand.

"Oh." Piper cringes. "That's...fun."

"And now we're going on a picnic, right Kate?"

I didn't say anything about a picnic, but once the girl has something in her mind, it's hard to deter her.

"Would you mind watching the store?" I ask Piper, finishing cleaning up the mess.

"Of course." She opens the oven and sniffs. "That smells so good. What is it? And please tell me it doesn't have zucchini in it."

I chuckle, remembering Piper's face when I told her that her favorite muffins had zucchini in them.

"Honey chocolate chip banana bread. Vegetable free."

"Can I have a piece?" Finley asks, bouncing on her stool.

"I'll bring some with us, but you have to eat something healthy too." I pull out the sandwiches I'd made earlier and put them in a bag with two apples.

She pouts but doesn't argue.

"Oh, I forgot to tell you that your mom called." I pull out the banana bread and place it on a rack to cool.

Piper groans. "She's been calling almost every night lately. Once she got wind that both Addie and Harley hooked up with some Alaskan hotties—"

I clear my throat and glance over at Finley who is

listening intently to everything Piper says. The kid doesn't miss anything.

Piper shrugs and continues, "Well, she's dead set on getting me married off. Thinks my biological clock"—she makes air quotes—"is running out of time."

"You're not even twenty-four." I chuckle.

"She was married with two kids by my age, which she never fails to remind me."

I slice the banana bread and add two pieces to a container, and then give one to Piper.

She takes a bite and moans. "God, this is good. You know you're never allowed to leave me, right?"

"Don't worry, it's not like I have suitors beating down the door for me." I place the container in the bag with the sandwiches, and say to Fin. "Go wash your hands and we'll go."

When she slides off the stool and races to the bathroom, Piper shakes her head. "I've told you a hundred times, you're gorgeous Kate. You just kind of give off this vibe."

"What vibe?" I cross my arms.

"The whole, I'm not interested in sex vibe."

I cough. "Are you saying I'm a prude?"

"A little." She grins at me and pops a piece of banana bread in her mouth.

"I haven't seen you out on a date since we've been here."

She shrugs. "Because I'm kind of on a man fast."

"How is that any different than me."

"Difference is *you* want the whole fairy tale, happily ever after. I don't."

I roll my eyes at her, but I know she's right.

"That said." She takes another bite of the banana bread. "For my stomach's sake, I hope your Prince Charming takes his time."

"Trust me, I don't think there are any Prince Charmings in this neck of the woods."

"No. But there are some really hot mountain men that could warm your bed until—"

"Can we go now?" Finley asks, racing back into the kitchen.

"Yeah." I take the girl's hand, hoping she didn't hear Piper's last comment.

"Have fun." Piper waves as we leave.

My thoughts are a jumbled mess as I walk with Finley, allowing her to tug me along. Piper was right, I do want the whole fairy tale, but I also want more of what I felt yesterday when Weston kissed me.

"Come on, Kate. Hurry up." Finley has let go of my hand and is running ahead of me, into the woods.

"Finley, slow down."

She doesn't, and I chase after her, wondering how the hell a six-year-old can outrun me.

"Finley, if you don't stop now, you won't get any banana bread."

That makes her halt in her tracks, and from the hill above, she turns and frowns down at me. "But we're almost there."

Out of breath, I huff the remaining way up the hill. "It's dangerous out here, Fin. You can't just run off. There are wild animals, wolves and bears—"

She starts laughing.

"You think that's funny?"

"Can I tell you a secret?" she whisper-yells.

I'm still trying to catch my breath. "Yeah."

She motions me closer. "My daddy is a bear."

"Yeah, you said that."

"No. Like a *real* bear." She makes claws with her hands and growls. "So are my uncles. But not me." She pouts at that. "Because girls can't be bears."

I sit down on a log and try to bite back the smile that tugs at my lips. The kid definitely has a good imagination. But I remember when I was younger, thinking my own dad was Superman. He always wore this t-shirt with the logo on it and would joke that he was the Man of Steel. At six I believed him, thinking he was the strongest man I knew.

"That's pretty cool," I say, playing along, not wanting to crush her fantasy that her dad is larger than life. Because I can understand why she'd think that. Weston was...everything.

Gorgeous, and all muscle, and not only that, he had a good heart. That was obvious considering the way he was with Finley.

I sigh, touching my lips, remembering the kiss.

"Come on, Kate," Finley says, taking my hand and tugging. "We're almost there."

"Where?"

"You'll see."

A few minutes later, we walk through the dense trees into an open area with a large gaping hole in the side of a mountain.

"This is it." She lets go of my hand and runs toward the cave.

"Finley." My heart races with fear. God only knows what's inside there. "Stop."

I only make it a few feet inside the damp, dark hole, when my foot catches on something, making me tumble forward. I hear the pop in my ankle before I feel the shooting pain that slices up my leg.

"Oww," I cry out.

"Kate?" Finley is beside me. "Are you hurt?"

Yes. But more than that, I'm terrified.

"We have to get out of here." I try to stand, but when I do tears burn my eyes from the pain. I bite my tongue on the curse that wants to rip from my throat.

"It's safe here, look..." She disappears into the shadows again.

"Finley, stay here."

She returns a few seconds later with a water bottle and a granola bar. "It's one of my daddy's caves."

I take the water bottle she hands me, and frown. "What do you mean, one of his caves?"

She sits down beside me and tears open the granola bar wrapper. "For when he's hunting with my uncles."

The child has a wicked imagination, but I'm starting to wonder if there isn't some truth to it. Why else would there be supplies hidden in a random cave on the mountain?

Still, even if it is the truth, it doesn't mean it's safe here. Because whatever Weston and his brothers hunt up here, roam these mountains.

"I need you to help me up, okay?"

In the darkness, I see her nod, but as I try to stand again, I know there's no way I'm getting down that mountain in this condition. More panic squeezes my throat, and when I swallow it's like shards of glass scratching their way down, because I'd been so caught up in my conversation with Piper, that I forgot to bring my damn cell phone.

Still, with Finley's help, I'm able to hobble to the mouth of the cave. As soon as the sunlight touches my cheeks, I feel slightly better, that is until I look down at my ankle.

"Oh God," I groan. It's already twice the normal size and a deep blue bruise circles it.

Finley looks at me with worried eyes when she sees my ankle. "I'm sorry."

I want to tell her that it isn't her fault, but the truth is she shouldn't have run off.

"Come here." I motion her to sit beside me, and after a slight hesitation, she does. "You can't run off like that. When you do, you can get hurt, or others can."

Tears gather, and her chin quivers. "I just wanted to show you the cave."

"I know sweetheart, but there are dangers up here, things I can't protect you from." And now I have no idea how I'm going to get her back to town safely.

It's not like I can send a six-year-old off in the woods alone. And it'll be hours before anyone notices we're missing. I don't want to panic, not yet. But when I hear a noise like something very large, very scary running through the trees toward us, I can't help the fear that paralyzes me.

That fear turns to terror as an enormous bear bounds through the opening, stopping when he sees us.

Oh. My. God.

This cannot be happening. Can't be the way my life ends. I can see the headlines now; **Stupid Woman and Undisciplined Child get Mauled in Random Bear Attack in the Wilds of Alaska.**

I have no clue what to do.

Play dead. Or is that only for some bears? It's not like I'm a bear expert. I'm not even sure what kind this one is. Maybe a Grizzly, considering the size. But aren't they the most vicious?

My mind races, and it takes less than a minute for my body to turn from flight to fight, but only because Finley jumps up from where she was sitting beside me and races toward the bear.

I try to snatch her arm, but she's too quick.

"Daddy," she cries out, happily, and I know that her wild imagination will be the death of us.

The bear looks at the child, then back at me. Good, I need its attention, maybe then Finley can run away.

Ignoring the pain that shoots up my leg when I stand, I pick up a rock, and throw it at the bear.

"Get out of here."

The rock bounces off the bear's side, and it doesn't even flinch.

"Finley, stop," I shout, tears now streaming down my face. She's only a few feet away from the beast.

The only thing that stops her is when the bear opens its massive jaw and lets out a growl that shakes something deep inside of me.

I hobble toward Finley, picking up another large rock, and tossing it at the bear. "Leave her alone."

The bear holds my gaze for a long second, and I swear I hear the words, *beautiful, brave, woman*.

It makes me pause, but only for a second. I pick up another rock and shout, "Shoo. Go."

I wait for it to charge me, but instead, it turns and runs back into the bush, disappearing in the maze of trees.

I collapse on the ground, my ankle finally giving out on me.

Finley still stands in the same spot, eyes wide, face pale. "He's...he's mad at me."

I can't deal with her fantasies right now. "Come here."

She walks toward me.

"You can't ever do that again," I say, my voice hard, no give to it. "Do you understand what could have happened?"

"But—"

"No, Finley. I'm serious. That bear could have killed you."

She frowns up at me but holds her tongue.

"We have to get out of here before it comes back."

"He'll come back soon. We just have to wait."

I pull her toward me, wrapping my arms around her and kissing the top of her head. "You're killing me, kiddo."

It's only a few minutes later when I hear more rustling, but this time it's echoed by two male voices.

"They're over here," one, that sounds a lot like Weston says.

"What the fuck are they doing up in the woods?" the other asks.

Weston grunts as he pushes through the trees, dark eyes piercing me with a look of accusation the moment he sees me. His brother Gunnar follows close behind him.

"Daddy," Finley calls out, racing toward him like she did the bear. "I knew it was you."

He picks her up and says something I can't hear in her ear. Whatever it is, it makes her face crumple in the closest thing to guilt I've seen from her.

"Take Finley home with you," Weston says to Gunnar, placing the child down. "I'll deal with Kate."

Gunner raises a brow and looks over at me. "Are you sure? I can—"

"No." Weston has his back to me now. "I've got this."

And the look he gives me tells me he certainly does.

CHAPTER 5

 eston

IT'S HARD TO FOCUS WHEN HER SCENT IS SO OVERPOWERING. Vanilla bean wafts around us as we trudge through the forest, over fallen cedar branches and through a path of wildflowers.

"I just need your hand, I can walk," she insists.

I snort, her petite body in my arms. "Like hell you can. Your ankle is sprained."

"I can't believe she ran off like that. I really thought I was getting through to her." Kate exhales, her head against my chest. Damn, it feels so right with her in my arms.

"I think her intentions were good," I say as we come to the clearing that opens up to my cabin, just one of the places I have in these mountains. "She wanted to show you one of our special spots in the woods, where she and I go for picnics. It's kinda sweet, actually."

I carry her past Fin's fort on the back patio and push open the sliding door, entering my house.

"You call that sweet?" she asks as I set her down on the couch. "A bear practically mauled us, Weston."

Clenching my jaw, I move the basket of clean laundry and reach for a throw pillow, placing it under her head. I wish I could explain everything without freaking her out. Truth is, I'm so fucking grateful we had already shared a kiss, because we are connected, bound in ways she doesn't understand.

Ways that saved her life.

What if another bear - a goddamn Grizzly - had been stalking those woods today? I run a hand over my thick beard, hating the thought.

"I'm just glad Gunnar and I were out and found you."

I so badly want to ask if my thoughts penetrated her mind - because hers sure cut through to me. That is how I knew to come find her and Finley - she was pleading for help. And I came to rescue her.

"I'm glad you were too." She shakes her head and I see a dark line of worry in her eyes. "I was so scared something was going to happen to your little girl…" Tears prick her eyes and my heart aches to comfort her.

"Hey, nothing happened. I found you, and look, you're both safe now." Sitting down on the couch beside her, I tuck a loose strand of her hair behind her ear.

"I'm the worst babysitter of all time."

I smirk. "Like hell you are. The last few days, since Finley's been with you, she comes home talking nonstop about how amazing you are."

Kate smiles softly. "My friends say the same thing about me. They were teasing me last night because I was googling recipes for homemade slime to make with Finley instead of working on my book."

"You're incredible, you know that?"

She swallows hard as if accepting those words is the hardest thing in the world.

"What is it?" I ask.

"I just feel like you're being too easy on me. Finley and I...we could have died today." Her tears fall freely now, and I realize how terrifying seeing me in my bear form was for her. "And Fin...she must be in shell shock. The whole time, she was thinking it was a game, minutes earlier she'd been telling me how you and her uncles were bears, and how you hunted by this cave - she had a whole story. Never realizing the danger we were in."

"It's okay," I try to assure her, wishing I could come out with the truth. But I know she's already had enough of a shock today. Finding out I'm really a bear might just throw her over the edge.

"It's not okay." There's so much guilt in her words.

"Finley has grown up in Alaska, so her sense of danger is probably a little off." I brush a tear from Kate's cheek, hating how torn up she is. "Let me get a bandage to wrap your ankle, okay?"

As I head to the bathroom for an ankle wrap, I try to clear my thoughts. Finley is fine, she's not traumatized. Besides, maybe knowing she's in big trouble when I pick her up from Uncle Gunnar's tomorrow will shake some sense into her. She knows better than running off to our family caves.

But Kate? She's really shaken up. I hate that my daughter's foolishness is the reason for it.

When I come back in the room, I'm amazed for the hundredth time by Kate's beauty. Her red hair is loose around her shoulders, wild and free, and her eyes are clear as the color of the sky on a summer day, the freckles around her cheeks and nose are so damn adorable, and I feel like the luckiest man to have this woman here, in my cabin - needing my help. She is way too good for a man like me.

"What is it?" she asks as I step toward her, slipping off her tennis shoe and sock.

"Nothing." I shake my head. How do I tell her that she's effortless and that is what makes her so damn attractive?

"Finley must be the talker in the family," she says with a tight wince as I access her foot.

"She's a chatterbox for sure. Takes after her mother in that regard."

I regret the comment the moment I make it. Why am I talking about Heidi at a time like this?

"She passed away, right?" Kate asks softly.

I nod stiffly, this is not where I wanted the conversation to go, but here we are. "In childbirth."

"I'm so sorry," she says, reaching for my hand as I sit on the couch and place her foot in my lap. "The happiest day of your life became the most tragic. How do you get over something like that?"

I go still, surprised by her willingness to go there. Most people try to apologize and move on, not wanting to go deeper. Not when it's about something so damn hard. It makes me respect Kate in a whole new way.

"I don't know if I'll ever get over it. But I've moved through it." I focus on wrapping Kate's foot as I open up, not quite believing I even want to go here with her. But when I'm with Kate, I feel like I can be honest. "Fin's mom and I, we weren't together when she got pregnant. It sounds bad, but I wasn't exactly looking for commitment. I slept with a lot of women and—"

"Broke a lot of hearts?"

I shake my head, embarrassed of my past. "I broke a lot of beds if that's what you mean. I was a player, Kate. And a total ass."

"So what happened?"

"It was a one-time thing with Heidi," I tell her. "One night changed both our lives forever. Sometimes I think about what life would be like if I hadn't met her. She might still be alive...but then Fin, she wouldn't be here."

Kate sighs. "That's a complicated reality to wrestle with."

"You know anything about that?" I ask, having the sense that she does.

"It's not quite the same, but I was engaged before." She bites her bottom lip.

I finish wrapping her foot and wait as she searches for the right words. I pictured Kate as this absolutely innocent woman. The idea that she has been engaged before shifts the way I see her.

"What happened?"

"He died in a car accident."

"Oh god, I had no idea, Kate."

"It's not something I really bring up. I mean, it's not exactly a happy story."

"Still," I say. "It's your story."

"We'd gotten in a fight and he left in a huff. If I'd been softer with him...he wouldn't have left. He would still be alive." She closes her eyes, her hand finding mine. I thread my fingers with hers, sensing she needs me to tether her to this moment. "I can't believe I'm telling you all this. I've never even told my girlfriends that."

"Hey, Kate, couples argue. People fight. His death is not your fault."

"I know that in my head...but in my heart? It's more complicated."

"Do you still love him?" I have to ask, I need to know where my mate stands.

She runs her finger over her lips. "With Matt and I...it was never about...I mean, it was...Matt was a really good man. He cared about me and I cared about him and I love that he loved me." She sighs. "That probably sounds strange. It's just—"

"You were never *in love* with him."

"Right."

Our eyes meet then, the moment is still, and I feel a heat rise from her. The same way I feel a need stir within me. She may have not been in love before, but this energy passing between us - it's real.

She takes a deep breath, the rise of her breasts sending a wave of desire over me.

"I feel like I've overshared," she says. "We were talking about you."

"No," I say. "We're talking about life." My brows furrow. "Can I ask you something?"

"At this point, with you, I think I'm an open book."

"You were – *are* - so young. Why would you agree to marry a man you didn't love?"

"My family loved him, and I hoped that would be enough. Matt was going to take over my father's law practice. He was my first everything and...it was safe, and I didn't know how to take chances."

"Do you now?" I ask.

Her lips tug up. "I moved to Alaska, didn't I? I quit my job to be here, decided to be a writer and threw all caution to the wind when Addie invited me on this adventure. So yes, I can take chances now."

"You're really brave, Kate," I say, running my hand over her leg, seeing her depth, and knowing there must be so much more to her than this. Wanting to know all of it. All of her.

"So brave in fact, I can stare down grizzly bears in the forest," she says exhaling, a smile finding its way across her pink lips.

"Kodiak," I correct. "It was a Kodiak bear."

She frowns at me. "How do you know?"

Shit. "Because this is Kodiak land. Grizzlies don't come down here very often. I just...assumed."

"I see, well then, I stared that Kodiak down. But you know what's strange?" she asks.

"What's that?"

"When the bear and I locked eyes..." She chews on her bottom lip, and I can see the hesitation before she shares, "It was like it spoke to me."

I laugh tightly. She *did* hear me. "Oh, yeah? What did the bear say?"

"Said I was a beautiful, brave, woman." She rolls her eyes. "Okay, I sound crazy now."

"No," I tell her. "It sounds like that bear knew what he was talking about."

She swallows, and when she speaks her voice is small. "You think I'm beautiful?"

I lean down, cupping her cheek with my hand. "Kate, you're the most beautiful woman in this valley."

Then I kiss her, knowing I won't stop there. Because it's the truth, she is the most beautiful woman I've ever seen, and lucky me, she's also my mate. And it's time I claim her as my own.

CHAPTER 6

ate

His kiss makes me dizzy with want. His lips part, his tongue finds mine and I open myself up to him. Well, that's all I've been doing this afternoon, but now it's in a primal way. A desperate way. I feel the heat rise inside me, my core bright with desire.

Weston's hands run over my body, my breasts are peaked with want as he gently caresses me. His gentle touch surprises me. He's such a rugged man that I expected his calloused hands to be rough, his passion greedy, but Weston is tender.

He kisses me softly, not in a pleading way. It's as if he is going to peel back each of my layers and open me up one petal at a time. His hands move under my shirt, my skin cool and his touch warm and I squirm under him, my pussy awake with excitement.

I haven't been with a man in so long. And then, it has only

ever been Matt. Matt who was timid and shy and predictable. Matt who only ever wanted missionary style sex. Matt who was a virgin when we met. We both were.

And now Weston. Weston the self-proclaimed player, who, by the sound of it, knows his way around a woman's body.

He pauses between kisses. "I haven't…" He closes his eyes, resting his forehead on mine.

"What is it?" I ask, fully expecting this hookup to end any second. Weston is ripped, head to toe, the sexiest man on this mountain, hands down, and he is winding his way into my heart at a speed that I know will leave me bruised.

"I haven't been with anyone since before Fin was born."

I lift my eyes in surprise. "Fin is six years old."

Weston nods. I feel his thick cock against me, and already my pussy is aching for his touch.

"Yeah, it's been awhile."

I close my eyes, feeling free to say anything at all to Weston. "I've only ever been with Matt."

"We don't have to—"

"I want to."

"Thank God," he groans, his fingers starting to tug at my clothes, tossing them aside.

I feel his need and it matches my own.

I want him.

Need him.

His own clothes quickly join mine in a heap on the floor.

I'm not a virgin, but with him, I feel like one, like my body is opening up for the very first time.

I moan against his mouth when he kisses me, wrapping my legs around his hips, lassoing us closer. Not even the pain of my ankle hinders the pleasure that fills me at his touch. And I want more. Want all of him.

He rubs against me, and the bare contact between my pussy and his cock is searing.

I thrust my hips toward him, wanting to feel his length deep inside of me.

"Want to take my time, sweetheart," he murmurs against my lips, but I can feel his control fraying. "Want to taste you, kiss you everywhere."

"And I want you inside of me," I say desperately, fingers digging into his hips. It's been so long for both of us. And I'm already wet, my body ready for him. "Please, Weston."

"Shit, Kate." He doesn't hesitate, his cock fills me with one good, long thrust.

"Oh God," I cry out, my walls clenching around him. He's bigger than I thought, and thick, and it takes my body a moment to adjust to his size.

"Did I hurt you?" He looks down at me, dark eyes filled with concern.

"No." I pull his head back down to mine. "It feels...perfect."

And it does. Everything about him is...right.

He begins moving inside of me, slow at first, building to a crescendo. My moans are frantic, and his own deep groans send adrenaline surging through my veins.

Our hips collide, his hands roam my body, and Weston kisses me hard.

My release is close, and I whimper, "I'm going to..."

"Come for me, sweetheart. Because I'm not sure how much longer I can last. You feel so damn good."

The roughness of his voice rouses my desire to a new level, and my body explodes in ecstasy. And at the same time, I feel Weston's own release, hear the roar of pleasure that vibrates through his body, straight into my soul like some type of claiming.

"Wow," we say at the same time, foreheads pressed

together, his full weight on top of me, making me feel...protected and safe.

Even though I know having sex with this incredibly hot mountain man is probably the most unsafe thing I've ever done - at least for my heart.

"Next time," he says, tracing my bottom lip with his thumb. "I promise to take my time."

Next time. I shiver at the promise in his words. But I don't know if there'll be a next time. There probably shouldn't have even been a first time, because I don't know how long I'll be staying here. And getting my emotions all tied up in this man is just...dangerous.

And, I'm not in the kind of place to have a relationship, especially not with a man like Weston Koleman, a self-proclaimed player who is out of practice … but I can only imagine what will happen now that I've opened the dam. He could start hooking up with any woman in this valley.

Plus, there's Finley to think about. I don't want to confuse her, and...

He pushes up on his elbows, dark eyes studying me like he can read my thoughts and he looks worried.

"I...we should go. Piper will be worried about me."

With a sigh, he rolls off me and starts to get dressed.

God, the man is beautiful. But this has to end today.

I take my shirt and pants when he hands them to me, but when I start to turn away, he takes my jaw in his palm and tilts my face so that I'm met with a pair of dark, primal eyes.

"I'll take you home, sweetheart. But let's get one thing straight. This isn't ending here."

CHAPTER 7

eston

No one has ever made me unravel the way Kate does. I shouldn't have read her thoughts, but it was like they were blasted into my head through a loudspeaker. And what I heard scared the shit out of me.

She's planning on leaving.

Can't. Won't let that happen.

She's my mate, and I won't let her run away. I may not deserve a woman like her, but I'll damn well fight like I do. And not just for me, but for Finley.

And for Kate.

Because despite all the excuses I heard her making in her mind about why we shouldn't be together, I know the truth, she needs me as much as I need her. I felt it in the way her body responded. Saw it in her eyes. She thinks she wants a damn Prince Charming to sweep her off her feet, but she's wrong, what she needs is a beast who will ravish her, push her body to the breaking point.

And I'm that beast.

But I have enough sense to know not to push her. So, instead of keeping her here in this cabin like I want to, showing her just how much she needs me, I pick her up, and place her in the old Jeep that's parked out behind the cabin and drive her back to her shop.

Piper comes rushing out when she sees me lift Kate from the car. "What happened."

"I'm fine," Kate says. "I can probably walk on it now, but—"

"I won't let her," I say gruffly, moving past Piper, into the bookstore, and placing Kate down on the couch.

"It's just a sprain."

"And you're a doctor now?" Piper says, crossing her arms, then she gives me a stern look. "Why didn't you take her to the hospital."

"Really, Piper, I'm okay."

"No, she's right. It looks like a sprain to me, but I'll send Rex Callister over to take a look."

I hate the thought of any man, especially another bear, going near my mate, but he's the town doctor and a distant cousin.

Kate starts to protest, "You don't have to—"

I give a low growl, and lean down, silencing her with a kiss.

Kate whimpers and Piper gasps behind us, and I can't help but chuckle at the shock on both women's faces when I turn to leave.

"Remember what I said, Kate," I say over my shoulder. "This doesn't end here."

I shut the door behind me, feeling my mate's confused emotions spiraling and mixing with my own.

There's a part of me that wants to press my own thoughts into hers, but I know that she's freaked out enough already.

Finley is playing a board game with Adelaide when I walk into her and Gunnar's house.

My brother hands me a beer and smirks at me.

"What?"

He shrugs, still grinning like an idiot.

Adelaide stands, placing a hand on her rounding stomach, and approaches, giving me *the look*, and I know I'm in for a lecture.

"Piper just called," she says.

"Oh yeah?"

"Yeah. And she said you kissed Kate."

I glance around her at Finley, who is now tuned into a cartoon on TV.

Adelaide follows the direction of my gaze, and lowers her voice when she says, "You know I'm going to have to sick your brother on you if you hurt her."

I chuckle at the threat, knowing I'd beat Gunnar in a fight any day.

"Don't have any intentions of hurting her."

"Just sleeping with her." Addie crosses her arms. "She's been hurt before. Just be...be careful with her heart. I've heard about your...pursuits."

"Not the same guy I used to be," I mutter, hating that I have to justify myself, but also glad Kate has a friend who will fight for her. "And trust me, I want more than to just fuck—" I bite my tongue when Finley glances over, then say when her focus is back on the show. "She's my mate."

"Shit," Gunnar says.

"Oh." Addie looks shocked, then her face starts to light up. "That's so amazing. Does she know? Did you tell her about...you know?"

"Finley did, but she didn't believe her."

"I have to go see her." She hugs me before turning and kissing Gunnar. "Isn't this great news?"

He nods, but I see the worry in his eyes.

"Addie," I stop her when she's by the door.

"Don't tell her, about the bear or mate thing. It needs to come from me."

She nods, before walking out the door.

"Spit it out," I say to my brother.

"Nothing to say. I'm happy for you."

"That's all?"

"That and you need to have a chat with your kid. She's going to end up exposing us all."

"I know."

THE NEXT MORNING, I MAKE A BIG BREAKFAST, PANCAKES, bacon, and eggs. Finley isn't an early riser, but the scent of the food has her pulling out a chair and rubbing the sleep out of her eyes.

"Why so much food, Daddy?" she asks.

"No reason," I say, knowing it's a lie. If I had cereal out for her, she'd be eating in front of the TV. And this morning, I need to have a talk with my little girl.

"Can you pour the syrup for me?" she asks, struggling to lift the jug of the freshly tapped amber liquid.

"Sure thing, sweetie." We dish up and she starts shoveling food in her mouth as if she has places to be. "What's the rush?"

"I just wanna get to Kate's."

"You're not going there, Fin. I have the day off."

She frowns, breaking a piece of bacon in half. "But what are we gonna do then?"

"I thought we could clean up around here. The cabin's a mess, in case you didn't notice."

Fin laughs. "You're gonna clean? Really?"

"Well, this place is a pigsty."

Her face lights up with a smile. "No Daddy, it's a bear cave."

The comment makes me set down my fork. "Hey, uh, actually, I want to talk to you about that."

"What?" She chomps on her bacon as if she doesn't have a care in the world. I love that about her. Her free spirit, I never want to take that away. But at the same time, she needs to understand that she's part of a special clan.

"We need to talk about yesterday. How you took Kate to the cave."

She twists her lips. "You're mad."

"I'm..." I run my hands over my face. Raising a child is so damn hard as it is. Trying to explain the fact that there is a clan of bears who want to take her from me isn't something I want her to know. But she needs to. "You know how your mom was a grizzly?"

She nods. "Yeah, I know. They're the bad guys, aren't they?"

"Not all of them."

"But some?" She's paying attention, and I'm glad to have captured that. I need her to hear me now, not run off again without a second thought.

"Some." I exhale, leaning my elbows on the table. "And Finley, when you run off like that, something could happen to you. I know you've memorized the woods, but Grizzlies are encroaching on Kodiak territory. That means—"

"Someone might try and take me to my other family."

I nod, realizing my little girl has probably heard way more than she ought to have over the last year. "It's not that I don't want you to know that side of the family, your mother's side. It's just I can't trust them right now. You are my first priority, Finley. My only priority."

"Kate though, she's yours too, isn't she?"

I frown, picking up my cup of coffee. "What do you mean?"

"She's your mate, right?"

I'm at a loss for words. I can't even begin to imagine how she knows that. And I'm not sure I want to answer her bold question. I lift my mug to my lips and try to think of how to respond.

Finley grabs a forkful of pancake. "So when will she move in with us?"

I almost spit out my coffee. "What? Fin, you can't talk like that."

"Why not?"

"Because Kate doesn't know about mates or about bear shifters yet. It's our family business. You need to promise you'll keep it that way."

She pouts. "But I love her, Daddy. Don't you?"

I swallow back my emotions, looking at my little girl who so clearly wants a mother.

"She's pretty special, Fin. But you can't make someone love you."

We work on our plates of food in silence for a few minutes, then she looks up. "I'll be seven in a week."

"I know, crazy how time flies, little one. What do you want for your birthday?"

She smiles as if baiting me for this question. "I want Kate to be my mom."

"Fin, I can't get you that."

Her face falls. Tears fill her precious eyes.

"I bet you can think of something else."

But Fin has already jumped off the chair and runs from the room. She pushes past the back door and gets inside her fort.

There I go, trying to make things work, and all I do is fuck them up.

CHAPTER 8

Harley and Addie enter Piper and my apartment the next morning carrying four to-go cups and an aluminum tray of cinnamon rolls.

"Where'd you get that?" I ask as they hand me a coffee.

"Well since you're flat on your ass," Harley says. "We knew there wouldn't be any fresh pastries or hot coffee in the cafe downstairs. So we had to stop at the diner for some cinnamon rolls to go."

"Thank you," I say graciously as Addie begins plating the food.

Just then, Piper sticks her head out of her bedroom door. "Oh my God, that smells so freaking good." She grabs the last of the four coffees and takes a sip. "Okay, that is definitely diner coffee."

I laugh. "You've gotten such refined tastes since you moved to Alaska."

"No," Piper says. "I just have a roommate who happens to be a world class baker and fantastic maker of lattes."

"Not world class," I say.

"Whatever," Addie says. "The Seattle Times did a piece on your cupcakes, Kate. There was a line around the block every day."

"Oh, and remember that reality TV show that asked if you'd be a guest baker?" Piper adds. "What was it called?"

"The Great Bake Off," I say, taking the proffered cinnamon roll.

"But that is ancient history," Harley says. "You're gonna be a writer now, right?"

"Um, actually." I exhale. "I think I'm quitting my book."

"What?" Addie's jaw drops. "What are you talking about? It was your dream."

I laugh. "I think fantasy might be the better word for it."

Piper frowns. "But you were so excited."

"I think I'm a reader, not a writer."

"But now you probably have all sorts of juicy things to put in your romance novel," Harley says. "You had a sexy kiss yesterday if I've heard correctly."

I ignore her by taking a bite of the roll.

"You have to give us more than that, Kate," Addie presses.

"You guys, it's irrelevant."

"Don't do that," Piper says.

"Do what?"

"Act like your life isn't worth talking about? Making light of the amazing woman you are, the things you've accomplished. You are always here for us. Let us be here for you."

Piper's words catch me completely off guard. They're so kind that I feel tears prick the corners of my eyes. Addie hands me a tissue, and everyone gathers around me on the couch. Harley is crossed legged on the floor, Piper is next to me on the couch, my ankle in her lap. Addie is in an armchair, leaning in. I am so lucky to have such invested friends. They deserve more than a half-told story.

"The truth is," I begin. "That kiss with Weston was everything. All the things. But it was also a bad idea."

"Why?" Addie asks.

"I have no business kissing a man like him." Or doing any of the other things we did yesterday. "Even if he's put his player-ways behind him, he's a father. He needs a woman who is here for the long haul. Me? I'm thinking about getting a ticket home."

"What?" Addie looks up at me with eyes brimming with tears. "You're leaving?"

I sigh. "I don't know. I want to bake again, but not just scones and muffins. I mean, I love scones and muffins, but—"

"But you're talented enough to work at the most premier bakeries in the country," Piper says, even though she's frowning.

"You're going to leave us forever, aren't you?" Harley asks as tears begin to fall down her cheeks. Gosh, what is with the waterworks? Addie, I understand. She's pregnant and cries at the drop of a hat. But Harley?

Wait. Harley.

"Are you pregnant?" I ask her.

Her eyes go wide. "How did you figure that out?"

"You're crying," I say. "You never cry like that."

She nods, happy tears filling her eyes. "We just found out yesterday."

We manage an awkward group hug. I can't get up because of the sprain, and Addie's belly bump is getting bigger each day. But it's a perfect hug nonetheless. We all exclaim over Harley's news, congratulating her.

"We weren't expecting it, but we are so thrilled," Harley says. "I'm still in shock, to be honest." Then squeezing our hands, she adds. "I'm just so glad I have you guys. I couldn't

UNTAMED DADDY

imagine becoming a mother without my best friends by my side."

I feel a knot in the pit of my stomach. I hate the idea of letting Harley down.

She sees my face and quickly shakes her head. "No, not literally by my side. I mean, emotionally here for me. Kate, you've got to do you, whatever that looks like."

"But also," Addie adds. "Maybe just take one day at a time."

I nod. "I can do that."

"And Kate," Piper adds, taking my hand. "I know losing Matt was so painful, but it doesn't mean you can't be happy now. I know you want to bake. But make sure that's the reason for you wanting to leave. And not because you're running from something or someone who could make you happy."

I blink back tears, gratitude swelling inside me for having friends who are so generous and kind. It's because of them I'm the woman I am today. And I wonder if Piper is right. Am I afraid of being happy again? Afraid that I'll lose everything? That I won't be able to go on.

Maybe.

Beside me, my phone buzzes. "It's Weston." I slide it open and read the text.

"What does it say?" Harley asks.

"He says he wants to see me. That he has a favor to ask."

My friends smile.

"A favor, huh?" Piper snorts.

I bite back a smile of my own. They don't know Weston and I have already slept together.

And truth is, I haven't told them because I want more. That's what scares me. Sure, it was quick, but I'd never come so hard in my entire life. Even now, the memory heats up my core, stirs a need, and I feel my cheeks warming, my skin prickling.

One more time. What could it hurt?

And even if I leave, at least it'll be with some memories that will get me through the lonely nights I know will follow.

CHAPTER 9

eston

I can't get Finley what she really wants for her birthday - a new mother in the form of Kate - but I'll do my best to make the day special for my little girl, nonetheless.

After we finish cleaning the cabin, the neighbor lady, Ms. Sandra calls and asks if Finley would like to help her with planting some bulbs in her front yard. Fin jumps at the chance, loving the idea of getting her hands in the dirt.

"Put on something you don't mind getting dirty," I tell her as she runs down the hall to her room to get ready. I realize it's a dumb comment. Everything Fin owns has busted knees and stains.

She comes back in a pair of overalls covered in grass stains, and I run a hand over my beard. "You want a new outfit for the party?" I ask her.

Her eyes light up. "I want a brown sweatshirt and sweatpants."

I furrow my brows as we leave the house. "I was thinking more of a party dress. Ruffles, ribbons, something like that? Why a brown tracksuit?"

She laughs. "Daddy, I want to look like you. Like a bear."

I sigh. Stopping in the grass halfway to Ms. Sandra's place, I rest my hands on her shoulders. "Sweetie, don't try to be me. Be you."

"But you're my hero, Daddy," she says. Her words are so sweet, so damn sincere, I feel tears prick my eyes.

Meeting Kate, making love to her - it has changed me. It makes me want to give both her and Finley the life they've always wanted. To be the best man I can be.

"If you want brown sweats, then you got it, sweetheart."

She stands on her tiptoes and tugs down my face, kissing me on my cheeks. "I love you Daddy, so, so much."

A LITTLE WHILE LATER I'VE STOPPED AT THE DELI FOR CHICKEN noodle soup and a bouquet of flowers. I don't know how to do this - the whole dating thing - but I sure as hell plan on giving it a try. It's not just a woman we're talking about here. It's my mate.

"Hey, Weston," a sultry voice calls to me.

I turn in the checkout line and see Kassi. I give her a bright, easy smile. Growing up together in Bear Valley, we've known one another for years. More than *know*. God, I remember one wild weekend we spent together on her boat seven fucking years ago. After Heidi, she pulled back, knowing I had other priorities, but I know Kassi has always held a flame for me.

"Hey Kas, how you been?"

She shrugs, setting her basket on the conveyor belt. "Oh, the usual, keeping busy with work. The fishing boats are out every day." She lifts a finger, pointing it at me. "But I hear you are even more busy."

"Come again?" I ask as the cashier begins to ring me up.

"Oh yeah," she says with a grin. Then she leans in and speaks more discreetly. "I heard your brothers' wives, Harley and Addie, talking about it at the diner this morning. They were getting cinnamon rolls and couldn't stop talking about you and their friend Kate hooking up."

I lift my eyebrows. Huh, okay, so now the entire town is gonna know I have a thing for Kate. Not sure what she'll make of that, but at least I've claimed her as mine.

"Anyways," she says, pointing a finger to my chest. "My feelings are a little hurt, Wes. You always told me when you were ready to date again it was me you'd call."

"Things change, Kassi. It's been a long time."

She twists her lips. "Sure, but we had a lot of fun, didn't we?"

I give her a smile. "We did have fun. But it's ancient history. This thing with Kate - it's the real deal."

"Really?"

I nod. "Really."

She smiles then. "Well good. No one deserves that more than you, Weston."

Her words surprise me, I don't know, maybe I thought she'd still have an agenda after all these years. "I don't know how it will play out. Kate is too good for—"

"Don't do that, Wes." Kassi shakes her head.

"Do what?"

"Start acting like you don't deserve love because of Heidi. What happened was tragic, but it wasn't your fault."

I know she's right, but there's still a part of me that wonders if her having a mate that wasn't me didn't have something to do with her dying.

Giving a small smile, I say goodbye and grab the flowers

and soup, then make my way down Main toward the bookstore.

It's been a long time since I've felt this way, the nerves that race, making my stomach twist as I open the front door of the shop and call inside. "Hello?"

Piper is there, a smile on her face when she sees me. "Thought you might be by."

"Is Kate around?"

"She's up in her room. You can go on up if you want."

I can feel the pull of my mate, and even from down here I can smell her sweet scent.

Piper chuckles.

"What?"

"Weston Koleman, are you nervous?"

I grunt, and walk toward the stairs, hearing the woman's laughter float behind me.

Sure, I'm nervous as fuck. The unassuming pretty redhead with eyes the same color as the sky has me all twisted up inside. My bear has already claimed her, and my heart wasn't too far behind in falling. But that doesn't mean she wants me.

I know her body does. That was clear when I'd kissed her, held her, filled her. She'd trembled, and quivered, and came so damn hard, I felt her pleasure in every cell of my body.

But I want more than just her body. I want her heart.

Her door is slightly ajar when I approach, and I see her sitting on the bed, a laptop in front of her, and her cell to her ear.

"Thank you, Markas, I'll think about it." She hangs up and tosses the phone beside her.

"Think about what?" I ask, pushing the door open and walking in, wondering who the hell Markas is.

"Weston." Her eyes widen when she sees me, then a small smile stretches across her sweet lips when she glances down at the flowers and bag I'm holding. "You brought me flowers?"

"And lunch. Figured you wouldn't be able to cook. And I've heard from Harley and Addie that Piper isn't the best cook."

She laughs, a sound that goes straight to my balls. "You're right about that."

I place the flowers and bag on the bedside table. "So, what do you have to think about?" I ask, returning to my earlier question.

There's a slight hesitation before she answers, "That was my old boss, he wants me to come back."

I frown. "To Seattle?"

"Yes."

My bear stirs inside of me. "And you're thinking about it?"

"I...I'm not sure yet." She closes her laptop and pushes it away. "I've realized two things since coming here. One, I'm a lousy writer."

"I doubt you could be bad at anything, Kate."

She shrugs. "And two, I miss baking."

"Then bake. But do it here."

The smile she gives me is strained. "It's not that simple. I was..." Her cheeks flame red.

"Tell me."

"I don't want to sound conceited."

"Kate," I say, sitting down on the bed beside her, needing to touch her, but knowing if I do that I won't be able to stop. So I keep my hands to myself. "You're the most humble person I've ever met. And I want to know everything about you. So, please, brag."

"She won't," Piper says from the doorway. "But I will. She's had articles written about her, TV shows—"

"TV shows?" I raise my brows, knowing I need to go home and do a full Google search on my mate.

Kate tosses a pillow at Piper, who catches it, then tosses it back.

"What?" Piper says. "It's the truth. You're the Queen of Cupcakes."

"So I guess me asking you to make Finley's birthday cake is a little under your league," I say when Piper disappears again, even though I have no doubt she's still eavesdropping from somewhere.

"I'd love to make her cake." Kate's face lights up. "And I bet I can guess the theme - bears."

I smile, despite the tightness in my chest. "Yeah. I was just going to get a chocolate cake from the grocery store and place a plastic bear on top—"

"Um, no way." Her smile brightens like she's already coming up with an idea. "I've got this."

"Thank you."

An easy silence stretches between us, and I try my best not to read her thoughts, but I can't help it.

Kiss me. It's a small plea, one I hear in my mind, and see in her eyes.

Sweetheart, if I kiss you now, I may not leave this room without taking all of you again, I push back without thinking and see her eyes widen.

Shit. I stand, knowing I just failed Mating 101. You don't press thoughts until your mate understands the full implications of the connection. It just makes things more complicated.

I need to tell her. But I don't want to give her any other reason to run. And her finding out I'm a bear, may just be the final straw that sends her running to the airport and away from Bear Valley forever.

"Weston?" she asks, her face drawn tight with confusion. "I uh...Did you..?"

If she asks, I won't lie.

"What?"

She gives a small laugh, then shakes her head. "Nothing. When's the party?"

"Saturday afternoon at my house."

"I'll come over in the morning and Finley can help me with the cake."

"She'd love that." I rest my hand on the door frame, struggling with what to say, whether to be open.

"I want to get her a present. Any ideas? What did she ask for?"

I rub the back of my neck and wince.

"Tell me," Kate says laughing. "It can't be that bad. As long as it's not a rifle or a—"

"She asked for you."

"Me?" Kate blinks up at me.

"She asked if I could make you her mommy."

"Oh."

"Shit. Sorry. I shouldn't have told you that. It's a lot."

"No..." She chews on her bottom lip, and I can see the war of emotions playing on her features. Hear her jumbled thoughts. "It's okay."

But it isn't, because I know I just freaked her the fuck out. I need to get out of here before I say anything else to screw up my chances.

"I'll see you Saturday," I say before leaving.

The only thing that gives me hope as I walk out of that bookstore is the one thought that Kate unknowingly presses into my head.

I want that too.

CHAPTER 10

ate

I'M NOT EXACTLY SURE WHAT I'M GETTING INTO WHEN I ARRIVE at Weston and Finley's the day of the party, but as I step inside their cabin, I'm pleasantly surprised.

First of all, it is much tidier than it was last time. No baskets of clothes and no dishes on the coffee table. Beyond that, the sliding glass door to the patio is freshly washed and I smell lemon floor cleaner on the hardwood as I set down my bags.

"I can help," Weston says, grabbing two of my totes.

"Be careful, the ingredients are in there."

"They're heavier than they look," he says, carrying them into the kitchen. "Are you sure you should be carrying that much weight on your foot?"

"It's much better now," I say rotating my ankle for him.

He looks up and down the length of my leg. Heat rises to my cheeks as he unabashedly checks me out. He gives a low whistle, shaking his head, and I know he likes what he sees.

"You look incredible in that dress," he says.

"I didn't know how dressed up to get for a seven-year-old's birthday party."

Weston laughs. "Do you know Finley? She's wearing sweats today."

I bite my lower lip. "Maybe I should have just worn jeans," I say, feeling overdressed.

"No," Weston says, shaking his head, and stepping toward me. He has me against the kitchen counter in no time at all and I pull in a sharp breath as his intoxicating scent overwhelms my senses.

I close my eyes, feeling his cock against my belly. "Wes," I breathe. "Not if Fin is here."

"She's not," he growls.

"Isn't this her party?" I ask as Weston's hands run under the hem of my skirt. My skin tingles under his touch. God, I want this man even though I know there is a ticking clock on this relationship. I gave Markus a tentative yes when we spoke yesterday.

"Finley won't be home for an hour, she's with her Grandma getting party decorations."

"Oh."

"So we have the house to ourselves," he growls in my ear, lifting me up onto the counter in one fluid motion.

I speak the first thought that flies into my brain. "We can't have sex in a kitchen. It's not sanitary."

He chuckles, looking down at me. He hooks his finger under my chin and our eyes meet. "That sounds like you plan on having a little fun before the party starts."

I exhale, my breath shaky. "No strings, no promises," I say, not wanting to give him false hope.

I'll give you anything you want, Kate.

I blink. Did he just say or think that? I shake my head, thinking I must be going mad. Weston repeats himself, this time no doubt his lips are moving because his voice is gravelly and filled with intention. "Anything you want, Kate. Anything."

"Right now?" I say, the need growing in my belly. "I want you."

He lifts me from the counter and carries me down the hall. A surge of excitement washes over me as I realize we are entering his bedroom. One large king bed dominates the room, and a rustic looking wardrobe is the only other furniture in the room. The colors are all rich browns and burgundies, masculine and so him. It feels intimate to be in his manly space, but also, as he shuts the door behind us, locking it with a firm hand, I'm able to relax a bit. The last thing I need is to be seen naked and straddling Weston Koleman.

And straddle him is exactly what I want.

We strip quickly, knowing we don't have a lot of time, and in seconds my dress is on the floor along with my panties. Weston has pulled off his jeans and flannel shirt and our mouths collide as fast as our bodies meet. Flesh on flesh, pulsing cock grinding against my needy pussy.

"God, I need you," he says, running his hands through my hair in a wild, untamed way that makes me feel beautiful and so wanted. So seen.

Makes me feel like I am his.

I swallow, not wanting to get my boundaries crossed, not when Finley is involved. So instead I focus on Weston's mouth. His lips. His tongue. We inhale one another, falling on the bed, he pins me down. Our fingers laced and his big thick cock between my legs.

"I'm gonna fuck you, Kate. I'm going to mark you as my own."

"Do it," I say, the uninhibited words released as he lifts my legs over his head, he fills my slick entrance with his throbbing cock.

The force is so delicious, so hard and so deep, I scream his name. "Oh Wes, oh Wes, take me. Take me now."

He does, he pounds his hard cock where it belongs, and the sex is rougher than I've ever had before. It is desperate and wanton and so erotic that when he comes inside me I gasp, the pressure undeniable.

He flips me over, holding my hips, tugging back my hair as his fingernails dig into my skin. I cling to the mattress, wanting to be taken in such a wild way. Feeling a surge from him that is bigger than life. Like a beast has taken control of Weston's body - a wild animal who knows how to make me submit.

"Ohhh," I whimper as his thickness fills me up from the backside. My ex-fiancé knew how to have sex - but he knew nothing about fucking.

Turns out, Weston knows plenty.

My pussy hums to life in a new, unbridled way and when I come, I claw at the bedsheets, my pussy aching for more. More. More of him.

He pulls out of me and I turn around, wrapping myself around him, both of us kneeling on his bed. I kiss him so hard, his lip breaks, and I don't stop there. I am awake in a way I didn't know I could be and it's like my skin is so hot, like I'm a wildfire burning bright.

"God," he groans, his cock still thick and my pussy still wet for him.

I push him down on the bed, straddling him the way I wanted the moment I entered his room. I lift my ass and sink down onto his cock, dropping my head back as I'm filled in a whole new way.

"It feels so good," I moan as Weston's hands move to my

hips. He rocks me, pulsing deeper into my pussy, and I press my hands to his chest, needing to hold on tight because this right here, is the ride of my life.

I drip for him, my orgasms rushing over me so fast, so hard, that I collapse against him as he is still coming deep inside me. When I press my forehead to his, I realize we never used a condom.

And for a crazy, insane moment I forget that I'm not on birth control. Instead, as I lie there in his arms catching my breath, I think, maybe I *should* have Weston Koleman's baby.

The thought is so ludicrous it pulls me out from the spell I've been under since the moment I walked into this house.

Weston has a way with me that is so fierce and loyal it makes me think and do out-of-character things. Like make love three times in a row.

"We should get cleaned up," I say, moving from his hot and slick body, trying to gather my thoughts. "Finley and your mother will be here any second."

"Okay," he says, sitting up and placing his feet on the floorboards. "But Kate?"

"Yeah?" I ask, grabbing my bra and underwear and stepping toward the bathroom connected to his master bedroom.

You'd look damn good carrying my baby.

CHAPTER 11

eston

IT WAS WRONG OF ME TO HAVE PENETRATED HER THOUGHTS like that, but I couldn't help myself. Knowing she was imagining herself knocked up, a full round belly, carrying my child? Damn, it got me hard all over again.

But my words scared her. With reason. She doesn't understand why I can hear her thoughts - and it's got to be terrifying.

When she steps out of the bathroom, I want to explain, but by then we hear the crunch of tires rolling over the gravel driveway and Kate is flustered enough with the idea of being caught having sex with me.

"Kate?" I say, taking her wrist in my hand before she can leave the room. "I can explain, later."

She shakes her head, confused. "I'm just going to pretend none of this happened."

"None of what? Any of it?"

"Wes, Finley's back. And this day is about her. Not whatever mind control game you've got going on with me okay?"

She leaves me alone in the room and moments later I hear her greeting my mom and daughter, but I know there is a false joy in her voice. I know, because I know her.

She is my mate.

And I've scared the shit out of her.

When my brothers hear, they're gonna be pissed. This is the exact reason we have rules. Why we have a council. Why we don't go rogue like the grizzlies, doing what we want, when we want.

People get hurt when that happens.

Like Heidi.

I strayed from the bear law before, and that choice left two communities reeling, never recovering from that tragedy. I slept with another man's mate, and now I'm stepping over protocol again because I want Kate more than I want to follow the rules.

I know I need to cool it, or I'll lose everything.

When I manage to leave my bedroom, having screwed my head on straight as it's gonna get, I find Finley and Kate already mixing the cake batter together. My mom is carrying in bouquets of balloons.

"There are a few more bags in the trunk, Wes," she says, cupping her hand to my cheek in greeting. "Do you mind grabbing them?"

Outside I take a deep breath, allowing the wild mountain air to calm my nerves. I'm all shaken up. It wasn't just the sex - the best goddamn sex of my life. And it's more than Kate being my mate.

I love her.

And if I'm going by her words alone, she doesn't love me back.

I wish I could shift right now, let the bear inside me out

to run free. Get some of this adrenaline out of my body before I explode.

But I can't do that now, not today. Instead, I reach in my mom's trunk and grab bags of food for the party. Dropping the bags of food on the kitchen table, I begin unloading them, careful not to catch Kate's eyes. I know if I do, I'll need to drag my fingers through her hair and explain my life away.

"Daddy, you okay?" Finley asks, breaking my trance.

"Yeah, sweetie, I'm fine."

"You don't look fine," my mom says. "You look worked up."

"I'm fine, okay?" I say, my tone louder than I would have liked and I see the flicker of surprise in Kate's eyes. If she's scared of me talking in a louder than average voice, she's really gonna be terrified when she learns just how loud I can growl.

"Why don't you get yourself a beer and go sit on the front porch?" Mom says in a tone that tells us this suggestion is not up for debate.

"Is Daddy in time out?" Finley asks her grandma.

"No, he's just taking a break, Fin," she tells her. "The ladies will stay in the kitchen and get the food ready."

"Yeah, Daddy, we got it," Finley says, her voice determinedly grown-up.

Kate chimes in. "It's true. We got it from here Weston."

I look around the kitchen at my not-so-little girl, at my mother who knows how to deal with men better than any woman I've ever known - she has raised her four boys after all. And Kate. The woman I want to spend the rest of my life with.

If there were ever a kitchen full of women to listen to - this is it. I grab a beer from the fridge and gruffly leave the house, feeling like the bear I am inside. Not the comforting, protective bear - but the one who needs to hibernate all winter.

I'm three beers in when people start arriving for the party.

My brother Gunnar and his wife Addie are the first to show up. Addie gives me one of her bright smiles as she walks up the porch steps, Gunnar keeping a protective arm around her waist that's already round with their child.

Jealousy stirs inside of me, making the bear even more restless.

"Kate here?" Addie asks.

"In the kitchen." My voice is strained, and I see my brother raise a brow at me.

Gunnar whispers something in his wife's ear and she gives a small sigh before going into the house.

He leans on the railing, arms crossed, waiting.

"What?" I growl out.

"You going to tell me what's eating at you?"

I take a deep swig of my beer then set the bottle beside me. "Just that I'm pretty sure I fucked everything up once again."

"Seems to be a Koleman tradition," he says. "Thank God we have women who easily forgive."

I grunt. "It's not just about forgiveness, it's...Kate's thinking about leaving."

"Leaving where?"

"Bear Valley. Alaska." I rub a palm over my beard and shake my head. "Me."

"Does she know she's your mate?"

"We haven't had that talk yet."

"Might be a good idea. Better than her finding out other ways." I see him wince and remember how freaked out Addie was when she first saw Gunnar shift.

But is there ever an easy way to break it to someone that

UNTAMED DADDY

you're a bear? Or that my soul is forever tethered to hers? That as far as she runs, I'll always be able to push into her thoughts and hers into mine. That I'll never be able to be with anyone else, because my bear won't allow it.

Not that I could imagine ever wanting anyone other than Kate. But if she leaves, if she finds another man to share her life with, there's nothing I can do.

Fucking pathetic.

Blaine and Harley pull up, and before my other brother gets out of the truck, I see his worried expression when his gaze falls on me.

Taking the large present from her mate, Harley says a quick hello before darting into the house. One thing about Bear Valley, everyone knows everyone else's business.

"Another mate crisis?" Blaine asks, knowingly.

I huff out a breath as our youngest brother Bennett walks up the path a cocky ass grin tugging at his lips. "You three look morbid as hell. Who died?" He chuckles and adds, "Or should I ask, who got mated this time?"

"Screw off, Bennett," Gunnar says. "You're just jealous."

"Trust me, bro. The last thing I want is to be tied down to some chick who can up and leave at any time."

His words twist my insides, confirming my fears.

"It's not like it's a choice," Blaine says. "One kiss and you're—"

"Which is why I don't kiss." He taps his temple, one brow raised like he's got it all figured out.

"What the hell do you mean, you don't kiss?" Blaine asks.

"No kissing, no mating. Simple math."

"All the women you've been with, you're trying to tell us you've never kissed one of them?"

"Nope."

"Bullshit," Gunnar adds.

"You don't need to kiss, for a good fu—"

"Hi guys," Piper says from the sidewalk, struggling with an oversized package. "Can't stay long, just wanted to drop this off for Finley."

Bennett hops off the step, taking it from her, giving her one of his smiles. "Hey gorgeous. Let me help you with that."

She rolls her eyes at him, but I see a hint of a blush rise up her neck and pinken her cheeks. Ignoring him, she turns to me, brows furrowed. "I've been trying to get a hold of Kate all morning, but she's not answering her phone."

"Everything all right?" Warning bells blare in my ear.

Piper, who never looks anything but poised, shifts uneasily. "Yeah. Just need to talk to her."

"All the women are in the kitchen," Gunnar says.

That seems to make her bristle. "And all the guys are out here, drinking beer. Figures."

Bennett chuckles. "Hey, Wes is the only one drinking. Which, by the way, seems pretty unfair."

Piper once again rolls her eyes at him, and when my brother follows her inside, I notice him whisper something else to her that has her scowling. The guy has always loved to push people's buttons, and it's clear he has a new toy. Unlucky for him, Piper doesn't seem like the kind of woman who enjoys being played with.

"Think I'm going to grab a beer too and check on Addie," Gunnar says, following them in.

When the door opens, I hear my mate's laughter float through, the sound going straight to my balls, but also making my chest squeeze. I can feel her emotions like they're beating on my own chest, but most of all I can feel her confusion, the unsettledness inside her that's the driving force of her wanting to leave - to leave me.

"Sure thing," I tell him, hating the idea of Kate's home being anywhere but here.

Gunnar was right, I think it's time I sat her down and

explained everything. The worst thing she can do is leave, which is already something she's thinking about doing.

"We've got company," Blaine says from his perch on the porch.

I follow his gaze toward a black Wrangler that's just pulled up to the curb, and the large, burly looking man who just got out.

Rynne Grant. One of Heidi's brothers. And a grizzly.

Fuck.

The man's got a small, wrapped box under his arm, and his blue eyes hold mine as he approaches.

"What the hell are you doing here?" I growl out, standing, and wishing I hadn't had those three earlier beers. "You're breaking the agreement being here."

"Wanted to see my niece on her birthday. No harm in that."

Blaine is by my side. "There is when one of your men tried to kidnap her last—"

"And whose fault is that?" Rynne says, not taking his eyes off me, his lips pulling back in a sneer.

I know what he means. Why he blames me. I blame myself. The grizzly who killed one of Bear Valley's citizens a few months ago, then tried to kidnap Finley, was Heidi's mate.

A sociopath and completely unhinged, he would have stopped at nothing to hurt my little girl if he hadn't been stopped. Now the guy was six feet under, and the grizzlies had another reason to hate us.

"You need to leave," I say, feeling my bear stir. My emotions are already heightened, my bear pacing, not sure how much control I'll have if the guy takes another step toward my property.

"Not trying to make a scene, man." Rynne sighs. "But that

little girl is my family, too. Heidi would have wanted her to know us."

That voice in the back of my head, the rational one, tells me he's right. But the Kodiaks and grizzlies have been at war for too long, and not just because of Heidi and me. This fight goes back millennia.

"Get off my property," I growl out, a sound that is more animal than human.

I see Rynne's own bear stir in his eyes.

He wants a fight too. Like all his brothers, he blames me for Heidi's death, and I know he'll stop at nothing to take my little girl away from me.

I take a step down toward him, and hear my brother's warning, "Wes, remember where we are."

In the middle of town, not in the mountains where we can fight like real men - as bears.

"You always were irrational," Rynne growls back. "Not sure what my sister ever saw in you. Warned her there'd be consequences. But she didn't listen. She'd roll over in her grave if she knew a damn Kodiak was raising her kid."

"This damn Kodiak is about to rip the larynx from your throat if you don't get off my lawn." Anger simmers hot inside me.

"If I didn't care about my niece, I'd lay you flat out right now, Koleman."

It's a challenge, one that on any other day I'd have walked away from. But today my bear is in control, demanding I remove the threat from Kodiak land.

I'm shifting before my brain catches up with my emotions. Clothes rip, nails turn to claws, muscles and tendons stretch and burn. Rynne shifts at the same time. And I hear my brothers curse behind me.

"For fuck's sake, Wes."

But the man is no longer in control, and teeth bared, I

lunge for the grizzly. We roll, claws and teeth sinking into flesh, growls and snarls echoing in the air.

Wild.

Untamed.

I fight with all the years of pent-up emotions and guilt.

Until I hear the women's shrieks, and my little girl's cry.

"Daddy."

"Get back in the house," Blaine demands.

Then a gunshot rings out, and both Rynne and I stop.

Bennett stands a few feet away, rifle in hand, face stern. "Enough. The both of you are going to expose us all." Even though it goes against bear law, he points the gun at Rynne, who is already shifting back. "You. Get the hell out of here now, or I'll have the council breathing down your ass."

"Fucking Kodiaks," Rynne mutters, gathering his ripped clothes, then walking stark naked back to his car.

I still pace in bear form, unable to gain control over my animal.

Gunnar comes out of the house carrying new clothes. Bennett is glaring at me, rifle still in hand, and Blaine looks like he's going to be sick.

"What the hell were you thinking?" Bennett yells.

I wasn't, that was the problem.

And as I shift back and look toward the house, I see a pair of wide blue eyes locked on me, hear the panicked cry in my head.

Oh. My. God.

Kate stands there, face pale, and I know I did more than just screw up. I may have just given her a final reason to leave.

CHAPTER 12

ate

WESTON IS STANDING BEFORE ME, PULLING ON THE SHIRT that's been ripped to shreds. Because he tore it off. Like a wild animal.

He *is* a wild animal.

No.

No.

No. I don't want to believe it. But I'm forced to. He stalks toward me and I step back, away, scared.

"You were the bear who came for Fin and me, in the woods, weren't you?"

He nods. "I can explain everything." Gunnar tosses his brother a pair of jeans and I look away as he pulls them on. "I told you I wanted to talk, this is what that was about."

"I don't want your explanations," I tell him sharply. "Besides, you were going to explain the mind control situation, not the fact that you can shift into a bear."

Behind me, Addie speaks up. "Kate, it's kinda the same thing. They go hand in hand."

I spin on my heels and hiss, "You knew about this? That Wes is ... is ... a bear?"

"The whole family is," Harley says, walking out to the porch. "The men at least."

"Your husbands they can ... they are..."

"Shifters," Addie says. "Kodiak bear shifters."

I feel dizzy, and before I faint flat on my back, my girlfriends guide me inside.

"You need to lie down," Harley says. "We can deal with that man of yours later."

I'm coherent enough to realize they are glaring at Wes over my shoulder and I'm trying to not scream over the fact two of my best friends have been in cahoots over this shifter situation.

"What else have you been lying to me about?" I ask as they lead me down the hall, away from the party. They stop at Weston's bedroom door, but I tell them to keep walking. I don't want to lie down on his bed right now. Nor do I want my friends to catch on to the fact that Weston and I very recently had wild, out-of-control sex in this very room.

They push open Finley's bedroom and I dutifully lie down. Not because they told me too, but because my head really is spinning. I turn away from my friends, frustrated and angry and so, so confused. As my eyes focus, I notice that there are posters of bears tacked all over the room. It's like a wildlife encyclopedia on large, furry beasts has thrown up in here. Oh god, Finley wasn't making anything up. Her dad really is a bear.

"Kate, don't be mad," Harley says sitting down on the bed.

I close my eyes and roll over to face them. Mad doesn't even cut the surface. But then hot tears fill my eyes, spilling down my cheeks, and it doesn't matter how upset I am for what they did or did not say. More than anything else, I'm just confused.

Addie's fingers run through my hair, soothing me. "When I saw Gunnar shift, it was so scary. It almost ended things between us."

"Me too," Harley says. "But remember when I was kidnapped and on the plane?"

I nod, of course I remember. It was a terrifying day for all of us.

"Well, Blaine shifted and his Kodiak strength is what saved my life. It made me less scared and more in awe. He's more than a mountain man, he's an untamed bear too."

They explain to me about being mated, how once it happens your partner can imprint thoughts on you, and vice-versa.

I listen, realizing that is why Weston knew I was thinking about having his baby.

"It doesn't happen all the time, of course, and never in the house. But sometimes the Koleman brothers need to let their bears free, they need to let them roam wild," Addie says.

"And you just let them traipse around the forest and sleep in caves?"

Addie smiles softly. "I don't want to change who Gunnar is. He is different than other men, but also more fierce, more protective, more ..." She bites her lips. "Well, let's just say when his bear stirs inside of him, the sex is really, really good."

I swallow hard, thinking about the unhinged sex Weston and I had earlier today.

My face must flush scarlet because Harley laughs. "I knew it. You've so slept together."

I shrug, neither denying or admitting to anything. "It just makes no sense," I say. "It's the stuff of fairy tales, not real life."

Addie grins. "We already talked about it, Kate."

"Oh yeah?"

She nods. "Remember? Your love story is more Beauty and the Beast than Cinderella."

I groan, realizing now what she was talking about.

A shadow moves by the doorway, and I catch Piper watching us, listening. Had she seen Weston shift too? From the look in her eyes, I know she did, and I also know she was just as blindsided as me.

"This is insane," Piper says, the fear I'd felt a few moments before mirrored in her eyes.

"Piper," Addie calls out as our friend darts down the hall. "Crap."

"I'll go after her," Harley says, jumping off the bed.

I hear some of the men calling out Piper's name as the front door shuts.

"We can't tell anyone about this," Addie says. "It would put them all at risk. Including Finley."

"Is Finley a shifter too?" I ask.

"No." Weston's mom stands in the doorway. "The women in our family don't shift. Only the men."

Addie and Elizabeth sit with me for a bit, until I'm able to stand without the floor spinning on me.

The guys are on the back porch in deep conversation, the tension obvious. But Finley seems oblivious to what happened as she runs around the backyard making enormous bubbles with the string bubble wand Addie bought her.

Piper and Harley finally come back in the house, but Piper refuses to meet any of our eyes, just sits at the kitchen table and takes the two-fingered shot of scotch Elizabeth offers her.

A few more people show up, including a few kids, and all talk of bears and shifters becomes hushed.

"The cake looks amazing," Weston says to me, as I finish the last of the icing.

I glance over at him, just briefly, but it's enough to have those damn butterflies taking flight in my stomach. Even with everything I know about him now, the attraction is undeniable.

We need to talk, the thought is forced into my mind.

"You," I say, pointing at his chest. "Need to get out of my head."

He gives a hard nod, then grabs a few more beers from the fridge before going out back.

"He really cares about you," Elizabeth says.

I hadn't realized his mom was still in the room.

"If I'm understanding the whole..." I whisper the word, "*Mating* thing. Then it's more of a physical response than an emotional one."

"You're wrong." Her lips twitch slightly. "Sure, the lust is a driving force, one I've never heard a woman complain about, but..."

My cheeks heat up at her openness.

"It's the love, the complete devotion, the bear's need to protect that makes it whole. Real. I didn't think my Weston would ever find his mate, but after Heidi..."

"Was she his mate too?"

"No. A bear only gets one in a lifetime. But I think you should ask Weston these questions."

I nod, knowing she's right. But also not sure if I want to know any more. It's all so crazy. Maybe the best thing to do is call my old boss back, accept his job offer, and hop on the next flight out of Alaska.

CHAPTER 13

eston

I'M GRATEFUL WHEN KATE STAYS TO HELP CLEAN UP AFTER everyone else has left. I expected her to leave with them. Wouldn't have blamed her if she had. What I did today, shifting like that, attacking the grizzly, it was careless, reckless. I'm lucky that no one other than Kate saw.

Except for Piper. That's a whole other mess. One that I hope Addie and Harley will be able to handle. But right now, I only have thoughts for one woman.

Kate.

She's in the kitchen washing dishes when I come in after putting Finley to bed.

I come up behind her and feel her tense. "You can leave the rest of those. I'll do them in the morning."

"Is Fin asleep?"

"Out cold the second her head hit the pillow." I place my hands on her waist and spin her around. "We can talk now."

She lets out a shaky breath. "I wouldn't believe it if I hadn't seen it with my own eyes. It's just so...unbelievable. So what is it? Magic."

I snort. "Isn't that what we call anything we don't understand?"

"You turned into a bear, Wes. Not sure anything will help me understand that."

"It's genetics." I lift my shoulders and let them drop. "I'm hardwired this way. Same as every male in my family."

"But not females?"

"No. Even though Finley insists she'll be able to shift when she gets older." I chuckle, but Kate doesn't even break a smile. "What else do you want to know?"

"There are more...people like you?"

"Shifters? Yeah. This is Kodiak territory, but we get the odd brown bear that comes into town. And then there are the Grizzlies." My lip curls at the mention of them.

"You don't like them?"

"We've been at war with their damn clan for generations. But my relationship with Heidi made things worse."

I tell her everything. How Heidi was mated to another Grizzly. How the man was the one who tried to hurt Finley. I tell her about the clan council, and about mating and the abilities that some have being able to read each other's thoughts.

Last, I tell her that she has a choice.

"I can't make you stay, Kate. If you want to leave, there's nothing I can do to stop you."

"But we'll still be...mates."

"Yes, but you can still move on, start a life with someone else."

"And you?"

I grind my back teeth. "Fin and I were fine before you came here, we'll be fine if you leave," I lie. Even though I know it makes me a selfish asshole, I add, "But I want you to stay."

"I want to be honest with you, Wes."

"That's what I want too," I say. "So tell me the truth, do you think there is any chance you and I ... that you could choose me?"

Kate dips her chin, a shy look on her face. It reminds me of the woman I thought she was before we got to know one another. She's loved and lost in the not too distant past and I don't want her to get hurt again. Not on my account.

"I don't know, Wes. The truth is, it scared me, you losing control today."

I run a hand over my beard, pacing the kitchen. "I know. I fucking lost it. But Kate." I turn to her. "I've never felt this way before. About anyone."

She blinks fast, and I see tears in her eyes. "I haven't either, Wes. That's what's so scary."

I want to pull her into my arms, swear my undying devotion - but she's not ready for that after everything that went down today.

"Can you give me a chance? *Us* a chance?" I ask her. "Give me a weekend, then decide what you want."

"I don't want to hurt Finley, have her here, seeing us ... test the waters," Kate says. "If it didn't work, she'd be crushed."

"Then let's leave. Go away for a few days. Focus on you and me."

"And the bear inside you?"

"He won't roam free. I can control him, if that's what worries you."

"You couldn't control him today."

"I was looking for a fight. Damn, I've always chased trouble, Kate." I drop my head, hating that she saw me at my worst. "It's hurt the people I care about the most. I'm so sorry for fucking up today."

"I forgive you," she says. She steps toward me, on her tiptoes, kissing my cheek. "I'll go away with you, Weston Koleman."

I lift my eyebrows, not having expected this, but damn, hoping I'd hear those words. "Yeah?"

She nods. "I was scared today," she says, batting her long lashes. "But also, I was pretty turned on."

"You were?" I clench my jaw.

She nods, licking her lips. "You, untamed … it stirred something inside of me too."

I grunt, stepping closer to her, wanting to pull her into my arms, make wild love to her all night long. But she shakes her head.

"Nope," she says, placing a hand on my chest. "Not with Finley here. When we go away."

I grin, shaking my head at this mate of mine. "Then you better pack your bags, darlin', because we're leaving in the morning."

CHAPTER 14

ate

I'VE NEVER BEEN ON A SMALL PLANE LIKE THIS, AND I SQUEEZE Weston's hand as his cousin Dayne flies us toward Anchorage. It's the biggest city in Alaska, and while I haven't exactly missed the hustle and bustle of a bigger Main Street, I love the idea of going somewhere new and exploring that place with Weston.

"You look nervous," he says - well, yells. We're both wearing headsets to block the loud roar of the plane's engine.

"It's a good nervous," I shout. And it is. I think Weston was right, we need some time without my friends and his family around, watching us. We need to see if we are compatible ... beyond the bedroom.

Leaving his house last night was torturous. My body was screaming to just pull him to his bedroom and lock the door and get down to business.

But sleeping with Weston is more complicated than that.

We have to consider Finley. Which is why when he called me at the crack of dawn this morning and told me we were catching a plane in an hour, I was immediately excited.

I want to give us a chance - I can't imagine walking away from Alaska if we have unfinished business.

My eyes are fixed on the small window to my left as the short plane ride passes quickly. Soon enough we're exiting the plane and headed toward a rental car waiting for us.

"It's weird seeing you drive a Prius," I tell him. "You look so much more comfortable in a truck."

He smiles, putting the car in reverse and heading toward the highway. "I'm comfortable anywhere you are, Kate."

His words send a jolt of warmth through my body. I like the idea of being someone's comfort, the same way I want someone to be my protector. Still, it also feels like a level of pressure on this relationship working.

"So where are we headed?" I ask.

"After we check into the hotel I thought we'd check out an Anchorage Food Festival."

My eyes widen. "That's today?"

"Yeah, today and tomorrow. Lucky, right?"

"I've always wanted to go," I tell him. "My boss always said it was one of the best food festivals in the country because it features so much local, sustainable food. It was kind of a pioneer in the whole farm-to-table movement."

"I didn't know all that," Weston admits, pulling the car up to a hotel. "I just thought you are into cooking and baking so …"

"That was really thoughtful Weston," I tell him, a lump forming in my throat. It feels so good to be considered. The idea that Weston wants to make me happy makes me want to make him happy too.

"You do?" he asks, grinning as he parks the car. "Because I

have a few ideas of just how you could make me happy if you were looking for suggestions."

"Were you reading my mind?" I smack him playfully. "Not fair."

"Hey, it's a two-way street, Kate. My thoughts are your thoughts."

I know the words are meant to give me a thrill, but they do the opposite. It overwhelms me. I care about Weston, but being his mate is a huge amount of responsibility. A huge commitment.

I'm not ready to make it.

We get out of the car and Weston takes my hand.

"I'm sorry," he says. "I'll stop reading your thoughts, I don't want to add any pressure to you."

I nod. "Thank you," I say. "Let's take our time, okay?"

He nods, leaning down and kissing my cheek. But I pull his mouth to mine. Kissing him deep and hard, my mouth parting, wanting him to know that I may not be ready for us to take things to the next level, I still very much want to be at this level with him.

"I can't wait to get you in the hotel room," he says between kisses.

But I shake my head. "First, though, we need to eat. I'm starved."

CHAPTER 15

eston

THE AFTERNOON PASSES QUICKLY, AND WITH EACH HOUR, MY need to be with Kate increases. God, the woman has me worked up. I try to keep my need for her under wraps, but every time my hand brushes against hers there is a rush of excitement that covers my skin.

It doesn't make sense to leave the festival after we eat lunch, so we spend the rest of the day loitering, hands held, taking in the sights. Eventually though, we need a break, our feet are killing us.

"Do you come to Anchorage often?" Kate asks as we sit in a beer garden at the festival.

"No, why would I? Bear Valley has everything I need. My family, my friends, my job."

She nods, seeming to understand. "You like being a guide?"

I run my hand over the frosty pint glass. "For the most

part. I have a deep need to be outdoors and taking tourists out in the woods satiates that to some degree."

"Right," she says picking up her pint. "You need to be outside because of the bear thing?"

"To some degree." I shrug. "But even as a man, I love the mountains. It feels like home. What about you, Kate? What feels like home to you?"

"I've always lived in Seattle, but my parents sold our family home several years ago. Now they live on a sailboat, they have a slip in the city at a marina. It's beautiful, but not exactly the kind of place you stay at for the holidays, or would ever bring the grandkids. It's too small for much company."

"Do you wish they hadn't down-sized?"

Kate shakes her head. "No, it was their dream. And we had a whole plan, really. Matt and I … well, we bought a big house on Lake Washington. The plan was for family holidays and everything to be celebrated there."

My jaw tenses and I set a hand on top of Kate's. "And then the plan fell apart."

"Right. We'd bought the house together, but after he died, I sold it. It was too painful, the reminder of what could have been."

"And then you moved to Alaska."

She nods. "Yep, after the sale went through Addie offered me this adventure. At the time everyone thought it was the perfect way to move forward with my life."

"But now?" Her words *at the time* echo in my ear.

"Maybe it was too brash, too fast. Maybe upending my life in every possible way wasn't the healthiest thing to do."

I stiffen, not liking where this is going. "You still want to leave? Move back to Seattle?"

"I didn't say that."

"Then what did you say?"

She runs her finger over the rim of her beer glass. "I don't want to have any regrets, Wes."

"And being with me, with Fin, you think you might regret that?"

"It's not about you guys. It's about my career."

"I like that your work matters to you, but I know who I am, what I want. Where I'll be for the next fifty years. You have to figure that out for yourself."

"How did you know, Weston, what life you wanted?"

"Look, before Heidi died, I was a mess. You know a bit about that. After Fin was born, things clicked into place for me. My priorities became crystal clear pretty damn fast."

"That's what I want," she says wistfully.

I pull back, confused. "What does that mean? You want someone to die on you again? Because I wouldn't wish that on my worst enemy."

"No, I mean, I wish I had an experience, something that pushed my doubts away, that gave me a clear, direct path to the life I wanted."

The conversation has a heavy tone. We finish our beers in silence and I wonder if the mood has gotten too somber or if we can still salvage the day. Kate must be thinking the same thing.

"Sorry if that got too dark," she says finally.

"It's okay. We need to talk this all through if we want to know where we stand with one another. With this relationship."

She nods. "Want to go find some dessert?" she asks, tucking her hair behind her ears.

"I'd love that," I tell her, taking her hand in mine, leaving the beer garden.

Walking around the food festival as the day comes to an end, we both seem to want to savor every minute we have together. It's almost like after the weight of the earlier conversation, we want the evening to be that much lighter.

We stop and try new items, talking to the vendors, I get to see Kate in her element. Her eyes light up when she samples sourdough bread with smoked Alaskan copper salmon, and she makes the most intoxicating sounds when she takes a bite of a red king crab cake.

It takes all my self-control not to place my hand on her back and lead her back to the hotel room so I can hear those sounds with her mouth wrapped around my cock. We may not know where we stand in this relationship, but it doesn't change the fact that this woman is my mate. And damn, I want her.

Used to Bear Valley where everyone knows each other's names, and the wild mountains where I can let my bear run untamed, I'm a little overwhelmed with how many people are here. But being here with Kate makes the crowds fade away. When we're together, it's like we're the only two people in the world.

"We still need to find that dessert," I say just as she pulls me to another booth.

"Oh my God, you have to try this," Kate says, placing a little sample spoon of wild blackberry infused crème brûlée in my mouth. "So good."

I take a bite, wrapping my arms around her waist and growl against the shell of her ear. "It's good. But you still taste better."

She laughs and kisses me.

I was never one for public displays of affection, but with Kate, I love it, happy to shout to the world that she's mine.

"Kate?" a man's voice calls through the crowd and I feel my mate tense before she turns to greet the stout little man with wire-rimmed glasses and a pudgy red face. "It is you."

"Hi Andre." She gives him a warm smile. "What are you doing here?"

He beams at her, obviously smitten with my mate. "Since my top pastry chef quit on me, I've been scouring the talent, and it brought me all the way to Polar Bear country. What about you? Last I heard you were working for Richard Chow. Quite impressive, but then you always were one of my best students."

"I uh..." She glances over at me, then says to him, "I'm not working right now."

"You're kidding me? A talent like yours. You could be running one of the top—"

"I needed some time off."

"Oh, right. I heard about your fiancé. So tragic." He places a meaty hand on her arm, and while it's only meant to be friendly, I bristle because I can tell he has ulterior motives.

The man is after my mate.

Or at least he's after her skills. I can see it in his eyes. It's only a matter of time before he offers her a job.

"Well, if you're looking to get back in the business I could use you."

And there it is.

"Thanks. I..." She chews on her bottom lip, then says, "I'll think about it."

My chest squeezes. I already knew she was thinking of taking a job offer back in Seattle, but this feels different. More real.

"Well, in that case, how about you join me on stage?"

"Stage?" She frowns.

"Another reason I'm here. Tomorrow I'm hosting a live stream of the Anchorage bake-off. One of our contestants just dropped out."

"I don't think..."

She hesitates, but I can see the excitement in her eyes, the desire to be a part of something bigger than herself.

She glances over at me. "I can't, I'm here with—"

"I'm sure your friend won't mind." He hooks his arms with hers and pats her hand while smiling up at me. "Would you?"

"No," I say gruffly. "Her *friend* wouldn't mind." Then, feeling like a selfish prick, I add. "Go, Kate. Sounds like fun."

"Are you sure?"

I give her a genuine smile. "Yeah. I'll be in the crowd cheering you on."

She wraps her arms around my neck, then kisses me, before Andre pulls her away.

CHAPTER 16

ate

It's after nine at night when we get back to the hotel and I'm a basket of nerves. I've agreed to a live bake-off with the premier bakers of the west coast, and I'm just now getting the email Andre sent over with the details.

"So I have to be there at ten a.m.," I tell Weston as I read the email. "Each contestant is given pantry staples, but we have to choose from one of the listed local Alaskan ingredients to make our specialty dish."

"Do you choose it before the show or during?"

"During. Gosh, so much pressure? Right?"

Weston comes up behind me, wrapping his arms around my waist and planting soft kisses on my neck. "You want me to help relieve some of that pressure now?"

I swallow, wanting to say yes. But also wanting to Google the other contestants, wanting to know what their specialties are before the show, so I know what I'm going to be up against. And I should brush up on local Alaskan ingredients to get some ideas for items I could potentially bake on live television.

"Your mind betrays you," he says, pulling back and moving toward his suitcase. Opening it, he grabs some sweats.

"I asked you to stop reading my mind," I say softly.

He moves toward the bathroom, pausing to squeeze my shoulders and kiss my forehead. "Kate, I didn't read your mind - but that doesn't mean I can't see that the wheels inside that head of yours are spinning."

I sigh, relieved that Weston respected my wishes. "That obvious?"

He kisses me on the lips before stepping into the bathroom. "I'm gonna shower, how about you order us some wine from room service? I have a feeling you're gonna be looking recipes up on your phone half the night."

I smile, relaxing. "Thank you for being so understanding. You brought me to this fancy hotel room and now my mind is all over the place. I don't want to let your expectations down."

"It's not just about the sex, Kate, being here with you. It's about getting to know one another, finding out if we're compatible."

"Thank you, Wes," I say, feeling the knot in the pit of my stomach unfurl.

Not knowing if it's because Weston is so gracious with me, or if it's because tomorrow I will be center stage doing what I love?

"You're going to be amazing out there," Weston says, rubbing my shoulders and kissing the back of my head.

We're backstage and the show is about to start, but funny enough I'm not all that nervous.

"Just be you out there and everyone will love you." He spins me around and grins down at me.

God, the man undoes me.

"I just hope the judges like what I make."

"This means a lot to you, doesn't it?"

"It's just good to be pushed a little bit." I chew on the inside of my lip. "If that makes sense."

He presses his lips to my forehead and nods. "It does."

"Showtime," a young woman with a headset says, clapping her hands. "Everyone take their places."

I lean into Weston, taking his strength, his affection, needing...him. But also wanting this. And I can't help but wonder if there's any way I can have both. But it's not like there are many openings in Bear Valley for a pastry chef.

"You better go," Weston murmurs, a smile tugging at his lips, and I wonder if he's read my thoughts again.

I start to turn to go, but he catches my hand.

"Kate." He brushes his knuckles down my cheek. "I want you to know that whatever you choose, it's okay. One thing this weekend has shown me is you're even more incredible than I thought. Smart, beautiful, talented. You deserve to have everything you want."

Everything I want.

Do I even know what that is anymore?

I stand on tiptoes and kiss him one more time, but the next thing I know I'm being pulled onto the stage, a thousand eyes on me, and my only thought is, *Weston, I want you.*

I push the thought into his head, hoping for a confirmation that he wants me too, but there's no response back.

"And we're live in ten, nine, eight..."

Frowning, I glance to the side of the stage, searching for

my mate. It's not hard to find him since he stands a head taller than everyone.

He tilts his head, and my chest squeezes at the sadness and acceptance in his eyes as they meet mine.

I want you, I repeat.

His lips pull up slightly, but the smile doesn't meet his eyes, and he pushes back, *I want you too, sweetheart. I just don't know if I'm enough.*

CHAPTER 17

 eston

"DADDY, KATE," FINLEY HOLLERS, RUNNING OUT THE FRONT door of my house to greet us. "Yay, you're home."

My mom follows her. "Did you two have a good time?"

I pull our luggage out of the back of the truck.

"Anchorage is beautiful," Kate says, glancing over at me uneasily.

I know it's my fault, the tension between us, my bear went and got all sullen and moody, and as hard as I tried to rein it in, insecurities and apprehension sit heavily on my shoulders.

"We saw you on TV," Finley says.

"You did?" Kate's smile falters slightly.

Again, my fault.

I wasn't surprised that my mate won the contest. Watching her on stage, her determination and focus, the spark in her eyes as she put the tiniest touches on each of her creations, she was mesmerizing.

Backstage, I'd even heard the producer mention that she should have her own show, that with her looks, and presence, she could be the next Rachael Ray.

"Did you keep the big trophy?" Finley asks, bouncing on her toes.

"I did." Kate digs through her luggage, searching for it, Finley hovering over her.

I catch my mom's gaze as she raises a brow at me, clearly aware of the tension between Kate and I.

"It's so pretty," Finley says, taking the faux-gold trophy that Kate hands her.

When she spins around with it, I say quickly, "Careful, Fin."

"It's okay." Kate stands. "She can have it."

"Really?" Finley's eyes widen.

You sure? I push.

Kate nods. *Doesn't mean what I thought it would.*

A touch of hope spreads in my chest, some of the heaviness lifting from my shoulders. But also guilt, because I wonder if my mood took away from her moment in the spotlight.

"Well, I should get going." My mom kisses my cheek. "I'm having a family dinner tomorrow night. I hope the three of you will be there."

"Thanks for watching Fin." I open her car door for her.

My mom has been an essential part of me not losing my mind over the past seven years, raising Finley alone. Because of her, I hadn't worried that my daughter was missing a mother figure, but seeing Finley these past weeks with Kate, I know I was wrong.

But it's selfish of me to force my own needs on the woman, especially if her needs don't match mine.

"Let me just take my bag inside, then I'll drive you home," I say to Kate, placing a hand on her lower back, needing her touch like I need oxygen. Wanting her to stay, but knowing I have to let her go. It has to be her choice.

"Can't she stay?" Finley pouts.

"I'll come back tomorrow." Kate places a palm on Fin's head and smiles down at her. "We can make a dessert to bring to your grandma's. How does that sound?"

Fin still pouts, tugging at Kate's hand. "But I wanted to show you the picture I drew."

I see Kate falter. "Okay, I can come in for a few minutes."

Finley is a bundle of excitement as she pulls us into her tent on the back porch. There are pillows and blankets piled everywhere and Kate goes along with it, climbing in. The three of us sitting in my daughter's fort as she pulls out her drawing, handing it to Kate.

"Do you like it?" she asks. "It's us."

"Oh, wow," Kate says, her voice is thin and watery. I try to understand why. "It's lovely."

When I lean over to see the picture, I understand why Kate has gone quiet immediately. It's a drawing of me in bear form, with Kate and Finley in the woods. Pine trees tower over us and even though Kate and Finley are drawn by a seven-year-old, it's still clear who is who. Kate has been given an apron like she wears in the kitchen, and Finley is in her overalls.

Kate is staring at the crayon lines and I see her blinking back tears.

Fuck. My mate knows what she wants, and I don't think it is me.

Not wanting her to cry in front of Fin, I take control. "Hey Fin, why don't you go in the house and get us a snack?"

"Can we have graham crackers and Nutella?"

"Sure, why don't you go make up a plate?"

She kisses me on the cheek and crawls out of the fort.

Kate wipes her eyes and I look around my daughter's fort, trying to collect my thoughts. All around us are tiny details of Finley's passions. A bird nest is in the corner, collected seashells are lined up in a row on top of an upturned cardboard box, a nature book on identifying paw prints in the woods. She is my little girl, through and through.

I love Finley with all my heart, I'm her daddy, and I only want a woman to step in as her mother if she wants it too, if she truly believes she belongs in this family.

"Want to tell me why you're crying?" I ask.

She wipes the corner of her eye. "I was offered a job," she says. "Andre wants to produce a show, with me as the star. It would mean me leaving Bear Valley—"

We hear a rustling by the door, and I want to ask more, but I don't want to discuss it in front of Fin.

"Finley?" I call out. "You need help?" There's no answer. I stick my head out of the tent. "Fin?"

Frowning I look at Kate. "I'm gonna check on her."

"Do you think she heard?" Kate asks, her face falling. "I didn't mean…"

"It's okay, she's a big girl," I say crawling out.

We look in the house, calling for her, but Finley isn't anywhere. The jar of Nutella is unopened on the counter and the front door is wide open.

"Shit," I say, panic crawling at my throat. "I bet she ran off."

"I'll go with you. She couldn't have gone far," Kate says, but I shake my head.

"No, you stay here in case she comes back. I'll go looking and will call my brothers if I need help."

I move toward the woods, shifting as I run, desperate to find my little girl. She doesn't understand the threats that lurk in these woods. I look over my shoulder and see Kate watching me as my body transforms into a wild bear, a Kodiak with the strength that could move mountains.

She was offered a job and is going to leave. Dammit, I knew she was too good to be true. Knew finding a mate would only lead to heartbreak.

But right now, I can't think about that. I need to focus on finding my daughter. She is my world, my everything. Even though I hoped and was foolish enough to believe that Kate would be as well.

CHAPTER 18

ate

THERE'S NO USE IN FRETTING OVER FINLEY YET, THE GIRL HAS run off multiple times before, and I have no doubt Weston will find her and bring her home safe and sound. So instead of worrying, I set to work on cleaning the house, because if I don't busy my hands, I'll let guilt busy my mind. If Finley heard my words and ran away because of them, I can only blame myself.

It's still daytime, so I focus on what I can do. Which is getting out the broom, rolling up my sleeves, and getting to work.

It helps to keep my mind off Andre's offer. And off the picture Finley drew of us. Two very different futures.

I just don't know which one to pick.

My career or a family with a man who makes my heart skip a beat and my body turn to mush. Money and fame or being a mom to a little girl who already has me wrapped around her little finger.

"I want both," I mumble, which makes me feel even more guilty.

But which future do you want more?

Weston and Finley, my heart answers immediately, even though it's the scarier of the two options.

I want them. This. Bear Valley. Even if it means giving up ever being a world-famous pastry chef. For them, it'll be worth it.

But as the hours go by, and the sun starts to set, and I still haven't heard back from Weston, fear begins to tighten around my chest. I call Weston, but his cell vibrates on the kitchen table. I try Addie, and she answers on the first ring.

"Have you heard from them?" she asks, answering my question if she knew anything.

"No." I chew on my bottom lip.

"It's been hours. Where could she be?"

The cave, my mind cries out. She went to her cave.

"I need to go," I say quickly. "I'll call you if I find anything out."

Have you checked the cave? I push into Weston's mind, right now glad for the crazy mate ESP thing we have going on and wondering why I hadn't thought about it sooner. *The one where you found us that day.*

I did, he pushes back. *It was the first place I looked. She wasn't there.*

But maybe she is now. I don't know why, but I have a feeling she's there. And scared. Like the child is calling to me. Not as strong as Weston's voice in my head, but still there.

We're on the other side of the mountain, we'll check again when we come back around.

But how long will that be?

Hours?

I can imagine Finley, knees tucked under her chin, tears running down her cheek, sitting in that damn cave, crying because she thinks I'm going to leave her just like her mom did.

I have to go to her.

Stay put, Weston growls into my head.

I don't answer back, because I know he'll only keep arguing with me. Instead, I go to his closet and pull out the gun I know he has stored, then with shaky hands I load it.

Once I'm out the door, I sprint through the trees, up the steep hill toward Finley's cave, ignoring the warnings I hear from Weston, because she needs me. I feel it deep inside my chest, like my heart beats with a warning.

The sky is dark purple and I'm out of breath by the time I finally make it to the cave. And for a second, I think I was wrong, that she isn't here, because there's no sign of her.

"Finley," I call out. "Sweetheart, where are you?"

Nothing.

"Please, Finley, we're all so scared—"

There's a rustling, then a small whimper from deep inside the cave. "You said you're leaving."

Thank God.

She's here, I push to Weston. *I found her. At the cave.*

I swear I feel his relief before he pushes back, *I'll be there soon.*

"Finley," I say, moving farther into the cave, remembering what happened the last time I was here, and faltering. "I told your dad that I was offered a job. I didn't say I was taking it."

More rustling, and then I see a small form ahead of me.

"You can't leave. You're daddy's mate. Don't you love him?"

I hear her real question...*don't you love me?*

"Oh, sweetheart." I reach my hand to her and she takes it. "I do. I love you both."

It's the first time I've really admitted it. To myself and out loud. But I know there's nothing that's ever been truer.

"I love you both so much," I tell her, meaning every word.

Her arms wrap around my waist and she buries her face in my stomach. "Then don't leave. Please, Kate. Stay and be my mommy."

My throat constricts, and I crouch down, meeting her gaze, and even in the dim light, I can see the spark of hope in her eyes.

"I want that, Finley—"

"Except you'll never be her mother," a deep growl-like voice says from the cave entrance. "You'll never be able to replace Heidi."

I suck in a breath. "Wh-who are you?"

"Finley, come here," he says.

"No." Her arms tighten around me.

"I said come here." His voice is low, menacing, and there's a threat in it. "I don't want anyone to get hurt. But it's time for you to come home to your real family."

"Kate," Fin whimpers.

"It's okay, sweetheart. I won't let him take you."

Weston, help, I push. *There's a man here. He wants Finley.*

Fuck. It's one word, but I hear the fear in it.

The man takes a step toward us, and both Finley and I move farther into the cave.

I pull out the gun from my waistband and point it at the man. My hands shake and I've never shot a gun before - but there is no way I will risk Finley's life right now. I can be brave and strong for her, for us. She is my family now and I will protect her.

"Don't come any closer or I'll shoot," I tell him, my voice steady though my heart trembles.

The man grunts, and in the shadows, I see him reach behind him. My instincts kick in, and I don't think, just fire.

Inside the cave, the gun sounds like a cannon going off. Finley shrieks beside me, but I know this moment of fear is better than a lifetime with the grizzlies.

The man collapses, and even though I can't see well, I know the bullet hit his leg.

"Bitch," he growls out.

"Reach for your gun again and I'll aim higher next time."

"I don't have a fucking gun."

I don't believe him, especially when I see the man shift before me. The already massive man doubles his size, and a loud growl fills the cave.

But he doesn't have time to charge before another bear barrels into the cave, slamming the grizzly into the wall.

"Daddy," Finley cries out and I pull her close to me, vowing to stay by her side for the rest of my life. Almost losing her shows me just how deeply I care for her. I may not have given birth to her, but I love her like my own.

Weston fights the bear for what seems like an eternity. Claws. Teeth. Growls. Snarls. They fight each other until the Kodiak has the grizzly pinned.

Two other bears pace outside the cave, as the ones inside shift back into human form.

"Stay the hell down," Weston growls, then says, "Finley, clothes now."

The girl moves away from me, deeper in the cave, and then returns a few minutes later with a few pairs of jeans.

Weston takes them and shoves his legs in one pair before looking at me and taking the gun from my still shaking hands. "You okay?"

"Yeah."

"Daddy, I'm—"

"We'll talk later."

She chews on her bottom lips and nods. She must realize how her choice to run away may have cost her life.

Weston ushers us out of the cave where the other two Kodiaks are still pacing. He drops the other pants in front of them before saying, "I'm taking Finley and Kate home. I'll let you deal with that slime in there."

"Weston—" I start.

His gaze is hard, angry, and it stops my words. "We'll talk later too. But right now, we need to get you both home."

I want to go home with you, I push, hoping he knows I've made my decision. That I choose him. *You're right, we need to talk.*

CHAPTER 19

 eston

WE NEED TO TALK.

I know exactly what we need to talk about - her leaving. Because after tonight, I'm even more convinced that she needs to leave Bear Valley. All that's here for her is danger. The fucking grizzlies won't stop coming after my daughter, and how am I supposed to protect them both when neither of them will heed my damn orders?

But I have to deal with Finley first.

"Do you have any idea what could have happened tonight?" I ask when we're finally home. Holding my daughter's stubborn gaze, I need her to understand how reckless she was. "That....man," I say through gritted teeth. "He wanted to take you away. He would have hurt Kate to get to you. Do you understand that?"

Tears form in her eyes and she nods. "I'm sorry, Daddy."

"Sorry doesn't cut it Fin. You've got to be more responsible than that. You put not only your own life at risk but also Kate's."

"I know." She hugs her arms around her small body and hiccups. "I was just so mad—"

"You can't run away every time you're mad or upset."

"But I'm not mad anymore." She blinks up at me, a smile pulling at her lips. "Because Kate said she'd stay. She said that she is going to be my mommy."

I frown over at Kate who's standing in the doorway. She gives a small smile, but it falters with my hard stare.

I turn back to Finley. "We can't make Kate stay here with us. It's too dangerous. And she has a job—"

"But she wants to stay. Don't you, Kate?" Finley looks at her with pleading eyes. "And I promise if you stay I'll never run away again."

God, the kid is good. But I won't have my daughter manipulating my mate into not leaving, no matter how much I want it.

"Finley, this isn't about Kate staying or not. It's about you disobeying me."

She frowns but eventually nods. "Okay, Daddy. I'll listen." Then says to Kate, "But you're still staying, right?"

"Yeah, sweetheart, I am."

Don't make promises you can't keep, I push into my mate's head.

I'm not, she pushes back. *I like it here.*

I glance over at her and the smile has returned. God the woman does something to me - makes me want so damn much.

My blood thumps in my ears, and I want to believe that she's making the decision for me, because it's what she wants. But after the night I've had I'm not naive enough to believe anything is as simple as that.

Finley insists on three books at bedtime, and I give in, not wanting to deny my little girl anything after the day we've had. There were a few hours when I'd thought...shit, I'd feared I'd never see her again. The scent of the grizzly was all over those woods. And even though I know my brothers will deal with him, that the council will put more restrictions on the clan, I don't believe they'll ever stop coming after Finley.

Kate sits cross-legged on the floor, listening along with Fin as I read the picture books. My chest aches at the simple, tender moment. The three of us together. It feels like a family. But I'm scared to give in to that feeling of hope because Kate and I still need to talk - without Finley around.

And until we do, I can't let my mind go where my heart already is.

After we get Finley to sleep, I make some calls, letting everyone know she's home safe, sleeping in bed. When I call my mom, my voice cracks. "I would have never forgiven myself if something had happened to her," I say.

"But nothing did happen to her, Wes. Your little girl is home. What you need to worry about right now is Kate. She shot a man today, Wes. You need to make sure your mate is okay."

Knowing my mother is right, I man up and head to the kitchen. Kate is waiting for me, sipping on a glass of wine. She pulls a beer out of the fridge and hands it to me.

"Figured we both could use a drink after today."

"Thanks." I take a deep swig, then sigh and pull out a chair at the kitchen table. "Today was pretty intense. You shot a man, Kate … are you okay?"

She sets down her wine glass, a line of worry in her eyes. "Loading the gun was scarier than pulling the trigger. In that moment, in the cave, when I felt Finley's life was truly on the line, I knew I was doing the right thing. It was weird though..."

"What?"

"It was like I could feel her. Not as intense as when you speak to me. Less and different, but I knew. Maybe I was just imagining it, but it felt real."

The connection she's talking about is rare, and usually only between a child and its mother, but with Kate, nothing would surprise me.

"You and Fin have a special connection."

She smiles. "We do."

"You're so brave, sweetheart. I know I said it was foolish to go to the woods alone, but your instincts were right. And they're the reason Finley is sleeping in her bedroom right now, safe and secure. I owe you everything."

She shakes her head. "No. It doesn't work like that. You don't owe me anything, Wes."

Sitting across from my mate, I look into her eyes, needing to know the absolute truth. "I know what you told Finley about staying, but—"

"Are you going to try and convince me to leave?"

"If that's what's best for you, then yes. You could have died tonight."

"But I didn't." She holds my gaze, and I swear I see my future there. "You're right about one thing. I am braver and stronger than I knew. And because of that strength, I know that what's best for me is right here. In this house."

I swallow over the lump that's formed in my throat. "And what about your career? Your TV show?"

She shrugs. "Some dreams are worth giving up."

"I don't want you to have to give up anything. Not for me—"

"Yes, *for* you. Because I *love* you."

"What did you say?"

She puts her glass of wine down and moves toward me. She sits down in my lap, wrapping her arms around my neck. This closeness is what I crave, her and me together.

"I love you, Weston," she says again. "And I love that stubborn, feisty little girl in there. And if you'll have me, I want—"

I crash my mouth down on hers, not letting her finish, because I'm too overwhelmed to hear any more.

CHAPTER 20

ate

I NEVER THOUGHT TRUE LOVE WOULD FEEL LIKE THIS, LIKE A weight being lifted, but it is. As Weston picks me up and carries me outside, I feel light as a feather.

"Where are we going?"

"I need to make love to my mate in the wild," he growls, reaching for a quilt that's sitting on a chair on the back porch.

My heart pounds with longing as he takes control. This is what I want in a mate, a husband - a man who knows exactly how to make me feel like his.

Cared for.

Protected.

Cherished.

The light of the stars overhead shines down on us as he laces his fingers with mine. We know Finley is sleeping soundly, her white noise machine lulling her to sweet dreams, and it gives us the freedom to walk to the large cedar tree in the yard.

Thick heavy branches filter moonlight as Weston spreads the quilt on the ground. He guides me down and I lay beside him, breathing in the darkness and the earthy smells of the forest floor. It's untamed land, and I feel Weston relax as we lie here, together.

He cradles me against his chest and I want to be naked in his arms, taken and consumed by this man who is also a bear. His connection to nature is so deep and raw that I can hardly understand it. But it is magnificent to see.

"When you fought the grizzly today," I whisper. "It made me feel…" I stop, the words feeling forbidden and vulnerable.

"It made you feel what?" He rolls to his elbow, using a finger to trace figure eights over my skin. When he touches me, it sends waves of want across my body.

"It made me feel excited. Hot … you were so … wild and untamed … it was erotic, Weston."

"You liked watching me protect my family?"

I swallow. *His family.*

"Is that what I am?" I ask. "Your family?"

He nods and blinks back tears that match my own.

"If you'll have me, yes. I will always be your family. Your lover, your mate. Your husband." He cups my face with his rough and calloused hand. "I love you Kate, and I want to share my life with you. Marry me."

Tears roll down my cheek and I say the one word that will change everything. "Yes."

He kisses me then. A kiss with promise and a kiss with desire.

Our lips part and his tongue presses against mine, I urge him closer, needing his body to cover my own. Not only protecting me from the world but also sheltering me.

This is not a summer fling. A one night anything.

This, what I have with Weston, is as real as this mountain valley. Will stand the test of time. This, what we share, is love. Real, true love. Love that lasts longer than a lifetime.

It is the kind of love that spans generations and can change the course of history. We slip off our clothes, not speaking - the words - the ones that matter - are the ones that have already been said.

And the rest can be spoken through our minds.

I love you so much, Weston.

And I love you.

I take hold of his thickness, wanting him inside me, filling me up. Our commitment to marriage frees up anything I may have possibly been holding back. His body is so strong, so chiseled, and when his hands run over my bare skin I pull in a sharp breath, the sensation of being with him, as his fiancée, overwhelming me.

My pussy pulses with need at the idea of being his wife. The mother of his children. His everything.

He must feel my mounting need, because he moves his fingers against me. Touching me so intimately and with a knowing flick of his finger. My clit hums to life as he massages the tiny nub. I bite my bottom lip, my knees dropping as I open myself up to him. My pussy weeps with relief as he gets me off so well, my back arching as he moves against my G-spot. I cover my face with my hands, so close to being utterly undone.

Your pussy looks so good when I spread your lips.

His naughty words send a ribbon of lust over me, unfurling against his fluttering fingers. I come against him, so hard that I let out a moan as the release covers me.

I want you to be my baby-daddy.

My thoughts cause a grin to spread across his handsome face and I reach up, pulling that beard to my mouth. I kiss him, hard, taking hold of his cock and easing it to my ready pussy.

His eyes seer into mine. *God, I want to put a baby in you.*

I bite my bottom lip as his cock deepens inside of me. It feels so good, so right, that I wrap my legs around him, wanting his seed inside of me so badly.

We make love under the moon and our foreheads press together as we rock in unison, the kind of lovemaking that can only happen when you've fully given yourself to another human.

When you've given yourself to your mate.

We move in harmony, and his cock is buried so deep inside me that I whimper, feeling the depth of his hardness at my very core.

When we come, the intensity overwhelms me, and tears rush to my eyes - I swear I've been crying all night. But our release is so overpowering that I tighten my hold against him, needing to be so close that I can hardly breathe.

I cling to him, and that is when I realize, he is also clinging to me. This love, it's equal and it's shared, and it is more than I ever imagined.

I love you, Kate.

Our pasts don't define us - the women he dated and the man he used to be. Just like my fear of stepping out in faith, taking risks, and saying what I truly want - those things shaped us into the people we are today.

Dreams change when we grow as people. And that isn't a bad thing. It's a beautiful thing.

"I hope you got me pregnant," I say, kissing the lips of the man I love.

"I don't need an excuse to keep trying."

We've both lost people that we cared about. But it has taught us something we will never forget. Life is precious and there are no guarantees.

When you find true love, you hold on tight.
You don't let go.
Instead, you go all in.

CHAPTER 21

 eston

"Daddy, look how pretty I look," Finley says, spinning around, her white bridesmaid dress twirling with her. I never thought I'd get my daughter in a dress, but then there are a lot of things I never thought would happen that have only been made possible since Kate has come into my life.

Like falling in love.

Like finding a mate.

Like feeling complete, whole, and filled with hope for the future ahead of us.

All of Bear Valley seems to have shown up for the wedding, including a very pregnant Adelaide, who waddles toward us, a stern look on her face when she sees Finley.

"You're supposed to be upstairs with the girls," she says, rubbing her extended belly.

"I wanted to show my dad how pretty I look."

"You look beautiful, like a real princess."

Finley beams up at me. "Wait until you see Kate, she looks like Cinderella."

My heart thuds like a drum against my chest in anticipation. I may not be the Prince Charming she always dreamed about, but this beast will do everything in his power to give her the happily ever after she deserves.

"You better listen to Aunt Addie and go upstairs."

Finley nods then follows Adelaide out of the room as my brothers file in, handing me a glass of whiskey.

"You ready for this?" Gunnar asks.

"Never been more ready." Everything has fallen into place. And even though Kate was adamant that she was willing to give up her dreams for me, I made a few calls, and a few purchases recently that will guarantee she doesn't have to give anything up.

"Have you told Kate yet?" Bennett asks.

"No, I'll tell her tonight."

"I still can't believe you're building her a TV studio, that's almost…romantic." Bennett laughs.

"It's not a TV studio, more of a kitchen workshop where she can stream videos of herself baking."

"She's gonna love it," Blaine says, clapping me on the back. "I think it's time to walk down the aisle."

Just then the door opens. "Weston," Piper says. "She needs to talk to you."

I frown. "I didn't think I was supposed to see the bride before the wedding?"

"I know, but she says it can't wait." She looks down at the phone in her hand and I frown.

"Are you texting her now?"

She groans. "No, sorry. That's my mom. Apparently, she's coming for a visit."

"That a bad thing?" Bennett asks.

Piper scoffs. "If you knew my mother, yes. She's obsessed with getting me married now that my friends are all hitched."

"Almost hitched," I say, feeling nervous for the first time all day. "What does Kate need me for?"

"I honestly don't know. But I'm sure it's fine. I mean, it's you and Kate we're talking about. You're the most ridiculous couple in this valley."

I can't help but feel a bit of pride over that. Since we got engaged, we've been pretty damn over-the-top with our devotion. My brothers thought engagement photos were tacky, but I loved it. It gave us an excuse to document the happiest time of our life. Hell yeah. They teased me over the fact that I rolled up my shirt sleeves and repainted the house, and that I remodeled the kitchen and bathroom - but damn, I wanted the cabin to be fit for my wife. Finley loved it, helping me install updated light fixtures and putting in a new washer and dryer.

I'll take ridiculous any day if it means the two ladies in my life are happy.

"Is she having cold feet or something?" I ask Piper as I follow her out of the groom's dressing room.

"I don't know. She wouldn't say. She went to the bathroom right before she got in her gown and came out all worked up." Piper twists her lips. "I'm sure it's fine. Maybe just nervous. She gets that way sometimes with lots of people. And this is a huge wedding."

"She wanted a big wedding," I say defensively. Kate wanted a wedding at a church, so of course that is what we are doing. And I'm glad it's not at my mom's place - she throws a good wedding and all, but I wanted Kate to feel like a princess today. My bride has been through hell and back when it comes to her journey to get her happily ever after. I want this to be her dream come true.

"Kate is in the church library," Piper says, pointing to a door in the hall.

I nod, running a hand over my beard - now I'm the nervous one.

When I step into the wood-paneled library, I lock the door, wanting privacy. Then I turn to Kate and smile - how could I not?

She holds a bouquet of red roses, surrounded by shelves of books. She truly is my beauty, in the library, and I am her beast, longing to devour her.

Finley wasn't exaggerating, she truly looks like a princess.

"My God," I say, stepping toward my bride.

She lowers her chin, looking up at me. I can't help myself - I need her in my arms. I pull her to me, her white wedding dress so beautiful, a bodice covered in glittering stones, the full satin skirt swooshing as I hold her to me.

"Tell me. What is it? What's wrong?" I ask the love of my life. My palm presses against her back, covering her entire waist. She feels so small in my arms, and it makes me want to be her protector, on an even deeper level.

"Oh Wes," she says. "I have to tell you something. I had to let you know before I said I do. Before any vows were made. I want you to know what you are really getting into."

"What do you mean?" I ask, bewildered. We've spent how many nights sharing every part of our stories with one another? It's impossible to believe there is anything about Kate that I don't know. She even let me read the chapters she wrote for her discarded romance novel … she trusts me with everything.

So what has she held back?

"I'm pregnant," she tells me. "We're having a baby." Her eyes dance with joy and I pick up my bride, overwhelmed with love for this life.

I kiss her, needing those ruby red lips against my own. "God, a baby?"

Her face shines with joy. "I know. I just took the test. I had to know why I was feeling so nauseous."

"This day couldn't get any better," I say, pressing my hand to her flat belly. Already imagining her growing my child.

"Oh yes it could," she says, a glimmer of excitement in her eyes. "You locked the door, right?"

I nod. "Yeah … why?"

She sets down her bouquet, and reaches to my belt, pulling down the zipper on my suit pants.

"Because I think I need a quickie with my baby-daddy before I walk down the aisle."

I groan. My cock ripe with desire as I reach for the hem of her dress. She laughs, there is so much tulle that it takes a moment to find her beneath all the fabric.

When I do, my hands cup her bare ass, the sliver of a thong granting me easy access to her warm pussy.

I lift her up, my pants probably wrinkled, but I don't give a fuck. Right now, I have my bride in my arms, her back against the library door. She sinks down onto my willing cock, arms wrapping around me.

Her pussy is tight as I fill her up, thrusting against my bride knowing she likes it hard just as much as she likes it soft. We come quickly, emotions mixing with pleasure.

Our faces could break we're smiling so hard.

I want to stay in this moment forever.

Kate hears my words and she nods, tears filling her eyes.

We have our whole lives in front of us.

A life that I never dreamed possible. But with Kate, the future is filled with possibilities.

"And babies," she says, reading my thoughts.

Yeah, sweetheart, as many babies as you want.

"Good, because I forgot to tell you that twins run in my family."

I chuckle, kissing her hard. That's a path we'll cross if we get there.

"But first, let me put a ring on that finger of yours." I'm grinning like a damn fool as I help her adjust her dress. "Because this beast can't wait another second to be married to his beauty."

The rugged mountain men of Bear Valley are ready to defend their untamed love.
Continue with the next Koleman brother's story in Untamed Fiancé!

CONTINUE THE JOURNEY

The rugged mountain men of Bear Valley are ready to defend their untamed love. Continue with the Koleman brothers' story in Untamed Fiancé.

CHANTEL SEABROOK

Amazon bestselling author Chantel Seabrook writes hot, steamy romances with possessive bad boys, and the passionate, fiery women who love them. Swoonworthy romances from the heart!

SIGN UP FOR Chantel's NEWSLETTER FOR LATEST NEWS! eepurl.com/bxqwB5

ALSO BY CHANTEL SEABROOK

Therian Agents (Lion Shifters)
Chasing Payne
Turning Payne
Taming Kiera

Six Men of Alaska (Reverse Harem)
The Wife Lottery
The Wife Protectors
The Wife Gamble
The Wife Code
The Wife Pact
The Wife Legacy

Full-length, Fantasy Reverse Harem
Cara's Twelve

<u>**C.M. Seabrook Books**</u>

Men with Wood Series
Second Draft
Second Shot

Fighting Blind Series
Theo
Moody

Wild Irish Series

Wild Irish

Tempting Irish

Taming Irish

Savages & Saints Series

Torment

Gravity

Salvage

Standalones

Melting Steel

FRANKIE LOVE

Frankie Love writes sexy stories about bad boys and mountain men. As a thirty-something mom who is ridiculously in love with her own bearded hottie, she believes in love-at-first-sight and happily-ever-afters. She also believes in the power of a quickie.

Find Frankie here:
www.frankielove.net
frankieloveromance@gmail.com

JOIN FRANKIE LOVE'S MAILING LIST

AND NEVER MISS A RELEASE!

ALSO BY FRANKIE LOVE

THE FRANKIE LOVE COLLECTION

New Releases
#OBSESSED
HOMEWARD
The Sailor's Secret Baby
His Old Fashioned
Dirty Cute
The Mountain Man's Muse
The Mountain Man's Cure

The Mountain Man's Babies
TIMBER
BUCKED
WILDER
HONORED
CHERISHED
BUILT
CHISELED
HOMEWARD

SIX MEN OF ALASKA
The Wife Lottery
The Wife Protectors
The Wife Gamble

The Wife Code
The Wife Pact
The Wife Legacy

MOUNTAIN MEN OF LINESWORTH
MOUNTAIN MAN CANDY
MOUNTAIN MAN CAKE
MOUNTAIN MAN BUN
#OBSESSED

Stand-Alone Romance
B.I.L.F.
BEAUTY AND THE MOUNTAIN MAN
HIS Everything
HIS BILLION DOLLAR SECRET BABY
UNTAMED
RUGGED
HIS MAKE BELIEVE BRIDE
HIS KINKY VIRGIN
WILD AND TRUE
BIG BAD WOLF
MISTLETOE MOUNTAIN: A MOUNTAIN MAN'S CHRISTMAS

Our Virgin
Protecting Our Virgin
Craving Our Virgin
Forever Our Virgin

F*ck Club

A-List F*ck Club
Small Town F*ck Club

Modern-Mail Order Brides
CLAIMED BY THE MOUNTAIN MAN
ORDERED BY THE MOUNTAIN MAN
WIFED BY THE MOUNTAIN MAN
EXPLORED BY THE MOUNTAIN MAN

CROWN ME
COURTED BY THE MOUNTAIN PRINCE
CHARMED BY THE MOUNTAIN PRINCE
CROWNED BY THE MOUNTAIN PRINCE
CROWN ME, PRINCE: The Complete Collection

Las Vegas Bad Boys
ACE
KING
MCQUEEN
JACK

Los Angeles Bad Boys
COLD HARD CASH
HOLLYWOOD HOLDEN
SAINT JUDE
THE COMPLETE COLLECTION

The Charlie Hart Collection

Daughters of Olympus

Their Siren

Their Mate

Their Phoenix

Their Shade

Their Goddess

Made in the USA
Columbia, SC
09 August 2024